"Gorgeously told . . . Through poetic, fast-paced narration, Bacon draws readers into her dangerous and exciting world to showcase the power of stories, art, and individualism."
—PUBLISHERS WEEKLY

"Lush prose twists and entrances, bringing Jasmin's harsh, regimented world to life. . . . Knowing in advance how Jasmin's efforts end in no way affects the story's power to surprise, horrify, and enlighten. Stories, after all, are more than their conclusions: it is the messages taken from them, and the actions that they inspire, that truly matter. *Mage of Fools* is a dystopian novel in which truth is the people's most potent weapon—if they choose to wield it."
—FOREWORD REVIEWS

"Eugen Bacon's unique vision, *Mage of Fools*, is a wonderfully imagined dystopia; a techno/folklore blend with a resourceful mother at its heart."
—Jeffrey Ford, multi-award-winning author in the fantastic genre

"When the final chapter of a book ends with the heading 'DENOUEMENT' you know instinctively that you are in the presence of a master—or in this case, a mistress of words! Armed with her all-conquering sword for carving unforgettable, lyrical and magical prose, Dr. Eugen Bacon has, yet again, delivered in her latest book, *Mage of Fools* . . . I'll leave you, my fellow enthralled readers, to discover the thrilling and gripping truth for yourselves, as you join me in praising this brilliant and powerful work of mind-blowing dystopian novel by the unrivaled Dr. Eugen Bacon."
—Nuzo Onoh, "Queen of African Horror"

"Bacon's sentences are ceaselessly reaching with a boldness that would have made Angela Carter proud. Her stories are restless and relentless. *Mage of Fools* is a clarion tale that examines the dangers of knowledge and, even worse, the withholding of it."
—Angela Slatter, award-winning author
of *All the Murmuring Bones*

"*Mage of Fools'* lush narrative, vivid characterization and expertly constructed world help signify why Eugen Bacon is one of the most talented writers working in speculative fiction today."
—Professor John Jennings, NYTimes bestselling author, and graphic novelist. Hugo Award winner for *Parable of the Sower: A Graphic Novel Adaptation*

"A brutal dystopia elegantly conceived with elements befitting legends and horror. A gritty world of politics versus community, the whole versus the individual. Bacon summons an African future where words and stories, folktales and memories, can subvert outside forces seeking to control the mind wanting to break free."
—Stephen Embleton, James Currey Fellow for African Literature, Nommo-nominated author of *Soul Searching*

"*Mage of Fools'* enchanting imagery and worldbuilding are richly woven in dark, delicious prose. This beautiful story reads like a dream trapped in a dystopian world with the texture of a fairytale. A poignant tale that has its characters dancing to its song with spirit, strength and some humor. I drank every achingly beautiful word."
—Tlotlo Tsamaase, author of *The Silence of the Wilting Skin*, Lambda Literary Award finalist and Nommo Award winner for Best Short Story

PRAISE FOR *THE ROAD TO WOOP WOOP AND OTHER STORIES*

"A commanding and visionary collection of speculative shorts . . . Complex, earnest, and striking, Bacon's impeccable work is sure to blow readers away."
—PUBLISHERS WEEKLY (Starred Review)

"Bacon's passion for language and her willingness to play with the short-story form, to never settle on one type of narrative or genre, make this an exciting collection that's well worth picking up."
—Ian Mond, LOCUS MAGAZINE

PRAISE FOR *CLAIMING T-MO*

"An instantly confounding and mysterious tour de force of imagination."
—Jason Heller, NPR

"Literate, imaginative, and provocative—a strong, even unforgettable, science fiction debut."
—FOREWORD REVIEWS

"Elegant and poetic language that pulls readers into each different world and experience as felt by the three leading women."
—LIBRARY JOURNAL

"Blurs the boundaries between genres."
—BOOKLIST

"A literary eloquence and decadence, which transports the mundane into the magical . . ."
—WEEKEND NOTES

Also by Eugen Bacon

Fiction
Chasing Whispers
Saving Shadows
Danged Black Thing
Speculate (with Dominique Hecq)
The Road to Woop Woop & Other Stories
Ivory's Story
Black Moon: Graphic Speculative Flash Fiction
Hadithi & The State of Black Speculative Fiction (with Milton Davis)
It's Folking Political
Her Bitch Dress
Claiming T-Mo

Nonfiction
An Earnest Blackness
Writing Speculative Fiction

MAGE OF FOOLS

EUGEN BACON

Meerkat Press
Asheville

To *family*
   My people.

For the stories we yearn to tell, the diversity of our voices.
   I am black.
      I am other.
         I am many.
            Betwixt.

PROLOGUE

It happens in slow motion. Jasmin runs inside the castle that stands atop a hill. She races up the winding staircase, hands moving along its mahogany rail shimmering with sheen. The Heidi dress she's wearing, a flowing thing that plunges down her waist and touches just above her knees, rises and falls with her running. No belt, just front buttons going down, down. She lights up a flight, up another, up, up. She rises with such thrill, such rush, all the way to the nursery in the northeast tower of the marble-coated monolith.

She flings herself into the rotary room—it slowly moves, revolves: a sundial or a snail-paced merry-go-round. It's a tavern with faint music in the background, an odd melody. The hiss of a snake, a soft clash of cymbals. Arched doorways, pillars rimmed with gold. Bracelets of orange-flamed candles at half-mast. Along the walls, dimly lit paintings inside veils of cloud, each with a version of the Garden of Eden: Eve leaning toward a behemoth serpent. Eve offering a glowing red apple to Adam. Eve and Adam running naked from an ash-haired god—a voluptuous woman full of breasts.

Jasmin catches sight of the children and her heart swells. Two-year-old Mia in her unicorn pajama set, tiny shorts and a T-shirt. Four-year-old Omar in his all-over flying dragon jammies. They lie on the floor, head-to-head, as the nursery spins.

"My goatlings."

Mia puckers up at the sight of Jasmin. Omar's eyes fill with reproach. Days and days of their mother's absence. She drops to her knees, throws her arms wide. The children yank out of their moment, soar within reach, fall into her breast.

. . . Pause.

Pause for a moment because that's not the beginning of the story. Rewind, back, back down the stairs. Jasmin tearing backward, down a flight, down another, down, down. Her rush, her thrill ebbing, as she moves away from the nursery, out of the castle with its white walls and white doors, mirrors everywhere. She walks backward along light-splashed lawns and their gardens full of bloodred flowers. She moves, not at a furious pace—just faster than slow. Back, back beyond the Ujamaa monuments of togetherness, sculpted hands of a village holding aloft a naked, black toddler with fat legs and plump cheeks. Back past the courthouse and its long windows, golden drapes in hourglass shapes, bound at the waist by melancholy ribbons. The courthouse splashed with lights from a trail of monster eyes hanging off the ceiling. A dais where the royals sit to give judgment. People go through the entryway peaked with spikes, they never walk out.

Rewind all the way to the egg shuttle—it has no wings—where you enter coordinates into the console and the vessel takes you for an intergalactic ride. The same shuttle that once saw the Neutral Zone, where you gazed at planets like Peridot and Tourmaline and they blinked brighter than jewelry. The shuttle that once lived in the land of Exomoon that had no shortage of xeriscape plants. Its wild blooms, cacti and succulents. Its sky of gargantuan rings by day, tiny moons by night. There, citizens changed color in more spectrum than chameleons.

Same shuttle that airlifts Jasmin to her execution.

Granite enters Jasmin's stomach as the vessel glides to height, then bullets forward. As the starlit night stretches into the horizon, Jasmin is a prisoner in a silent egg in the sky. She looks down and sees the people of Ujamaa Village in a gather. They gaze up at the egg flickering with incandescent lights as it climbs higher into the skyline with its cargo. Jasmin wonders if, on the face of it, despite the crowd's helplessness, some question what dies, what lives, and the power of a crowd. She wonders if, one day, a turning point will swing without warning in Mafinga. And when that happens if the same mob—that now stands with limp hands and gazes with bleak eyes at dusk and the egg soaring up the sky toward its scatter of stars—will reach the edge of its stupor, finally tremble and come to life in a murmur that lights to a roar.

JASMIN

1

Tuesday.

Outside the double-glazed window, a speck grows from the moonless night and yawns wide, wider, until its luster washes into the single-roomed space, rectangular and monolithic. One could mistake the room for a cargo container.

The space, one of many units neatly rowed and paralleled in Ujamaa Village, pulses for a moment as the radiance outside grows with its flicker of green, yellow and bronze. The cocktail of incandescent light tugs along a tail of heat. Both light and heat seep through the walls of the khaki-colored shelter, whose metallic sheen is a fabrication, not at all metal.

Light through the window on the short face of the house—the side that gazes toward Central District in the distance—rests on the luminous faces of a mother and her two young children, their eyes pale with deficiency in a ravaged world. It's a world of citizens packed as goods in units whose short faces all stare toward the Central District that will shortly awaken in the dead of the night. The light drowns the toddler's cry of wonder.

As sudden as the ray's emergence, it evanesces and snatches away its radiance, leaving behind hoarfrost silence. A sound unscrolls itself from the darkness outside. First, it's a thunderhead writing itself through desert country—because this world is dry and naked, barren as its queen.

The lone cry of a wounded creature, a howl or a wail reminiscent of the screech of a black-capped owl, plaintive yet soulful, rises above the flat roofs screening the wasted village. The cry is a dirge that tells an often-story of someone in agony, of a hand stretched out to touch an angel of saving but never reaches. A second thunderhead slits the sound midcry, nobody can save the mortally wounded one.

Jasmin closes her eyes. She needs no one to tell her. She knows.

Everybody knows—except the children. That King Magu's guards—so few of them, yet so deadly—have found another story machine, and its reader.

2

"Siyent yight," says two-year-old Mia. Her owl eyes—evolved to navigate darkness—gaze into Jasmin's. But they are eyes that are also glows: they not only see but soak light to illuminate her world.

Jasmin does not speak. She's unpacking the reality of what's just happened. She is overwhelmed by an emotion that's not yet rage. Her ears are ringing, a child's sound toy, but there are no more toys in Mafinga. The country's reality is cold, gray. Its wind vibrates with the dirge of a better yesterday. It's a world gone dumb—must all be broken? The bones of the ancestors pop with metamorphic hymns of water that is ruler and land that is slave, as people degenerate into crustaceans.

"Siyent yight, Mamm," says Mia again.

Jasmin's fingers rest on Mia's twin cornrows that end in pigtails.

"Yes. The silent lights."

"Someone hurt?"

Jasmin is taken aback. She never imagined Mia understood.

"The sirens are coming," says Omar in his grown-up voice. Even at four, he hasn't outgrown the burst of curls on his head. His pale chocolate skin is still baby soft.

"Soon," says Jasmin. "You know what it means."

She glances at the children still hugged to her hips. They too are readers, partaking of the story machine, they just don't know it yet. Each time she narrates from the device—

She closes her eyes, unwilling to fathom how much she has endangered them with her oral tales.

"I bwashed my teeff."

"Good, Mia. Now you, Omar. Make it happen."

He peels himself from gazing at the world out there.

Mia stays. Her eyes seek assurance. "I good, Mamm, aight?"

"You're always good, dear goatling."

The children know about goats. The goats from the stories Jasmin tells them. Tales of animals so calm, you think they are stupid, but their working minds sharpen with each bleat. Despite their odd pupil shape, how unsettling to a human eye, goats are intelligent beneath the horn.

Jasmin watches as Omar navigates the space between the unpartitioned living area with its metal-like seats and spartan table, its kitchenette with a tiny chiller and microwave, its multipurpose sink, the sleeping area with its floored mattress, its toilet—only a curtain for privacy. One wall is fitted with an automated screen that turns itself on, off at central command. You don't flick channels to choose the news, sports, documentaries, music or entertainment. *Pzzz. Pzzz.* The screen comes on at a whim with the propaganda of the moment: sometimes it's a choir of children in flowing pinafores and jester pantaloons singing slogans. Or the same children in sisal skirts and war paint doing a folk dance, chanting the *Hau, Hau, Acha We* song about decrying dissenters. *Pzzz. Pzzz.* The screen goes silent as it does now, momentarily asleep.

All units in Ujamaa Village are the same. They are metallic khaki in color. Everyone's within a kick, right there, next door. But you never hear anything—except the outside. And, mostly, as just then, the outside world brings the sound of dying.

Once a week you get a pass to use the Ujamaa Facility. It used to have gendered showers: hot sizzles and soap dispensers, a luxury despite the blandness of their products. But there are no more men in the village. Now the sizzler showers and their weekly extravagance are for everyone. There's no place for modesty.

Whoop. Whoop. The work siren goes.

3

Doors open, doors close.

The citizens of Mafinga respond in unison to the siren. They file out, headed to labor in Central District. Preallocated duties at Ujamaa Factory, Ujamaa Tech, Ujamaa Medico, Ujamaa Yaya and many other Ujamaas await them. The lucky ones, specially favored for an aptitude toward loyalty to the king, serve as guards and supervisors, and return home to snug two-roomers. The skilled ones, Solo and her mates, are also lucky. They live and work in the king's mines—away from guards and supervisors, away from fear and indignity of day-by-day oppression. The skilled ones are entrusted with drilling mafinite, a gem equal in value to a diamond. But even they are not exempt from a major trait of the king's paranoia: freedom. They are bound by location and need special permits to leave the mines.

When did it come to this? wonders Jasmin as she and the children exit the room.

They join the sea of bodies, a human march at night-break. Only a fool would leave shelter by day. But you had to see who died, how they died, in the sick bays of Ujamaa Medico to know it wasn't a good idea to brave daylight.

It's too dark to see who's there, bodies clustered in compulsory obedience to community service. They are wrapped in thermals, scarves, threaded coats much thinned from nightly wind. Sometimes, as she walks, Jasmin makes out smells: fresh soap or unwash, but often it's the stench of despair.

She firmly holds Omar and Mia's gloved hands. She pushes with them, and a few other mothers and their small children, as they head, first on instinct and then guided by glimmer—the growing flicker of Mama Gambo's unit. They plow toward the edge of the crowd.

Mama Gambo is a collector. She gathers the young ones, delivers them to a place past what was once an old church, now yawning cobwebs. She takes the children to Ujamaa Yaya. There, children learn slogans, as teachers filter out proclivity to loyalty (these make guards or supervisors), intelligence (these make the king's miners) or a trade (these make workers).

Jasmin and the children are the first to reach Mama Gambo.

"My little soldiers," the older woman says.

"Don't make warriors of my children," says Jasmin.

Mama Gambo doesn't answer immediately. She smiles at Mia, then Omar. There's kindness in the shape of her lips, the touch of her fingers. Her expression stays the same when, finally, she looks at Jasmin. "Someone's holding a fart."

"More like constipation," says Jasmin.

"I can see how that would make you sour. Now an enema . . ."

"Is a luxury that's an enemy of the state."

"The king and queen live in luxury up the hill."

"How is that equality?"

"Be careful. People are coming." Mama Gambo lowers her voice. "It's treason to simply speak of those slayers."

"They are worse than slayers."

"But you can't cut a thorn tree with a twig. Patience." Mama Gambo looks at Mia and Omar. "For these ones. Otherwise all we give them is regret."

"I thank your kindness to the little ones." Jasmin's voice is gentler. She turns to the children. "Be good, my goatlings."

"Aight," says Mia.

"Mama," says Omar. "It doesn't take much to see we're not baby goats."

"You certainly aren't, my lambs."

"Please, Mama."

She knows she's wrong to call him a lamb. He's not meek, never quiet, but he is gentle. The word is an endearment for his innocence and sweetness.

"On my way, then." But she doesn't leave.

Mia is picking her nose and sucking her forefinger. Jasmin doesn't snap at her to stop, as she normally would. Instead, she touches the crowns of her children's heads as if each was embossed in braille. Her heart is lacerated, torn each night, every moment she must leave them. She's always known their destinies remain uncertain, still even now she strains to read with her fingers the nonfiction of their tomorrows.

But their eyes gazing into her own tell a different narrative that is too deeply etched into their cores for fathoming. Their stories needle and wheedle into her anguish, her longing. She seeks to prophesy better fortunes for them but, right this moment, her vision is impaired.

She reads nothing in the imaginary bumps and cells in the cornrows and curls, just words in her own head that swirl in a language of Babel, a deliberate confusion of the gods. There are no allies or mentors, just tricksters and shifters, enemies and ordeals that dangle death, never rebirth. There's no road to resurrection, nothing that lifts with the precision of genetics, just her sweat-drenched fingers from the crowns of their heads.

"Go. My daughter," says Mama Gambo.

"But she's not your daughter . . ." begins Omar.

"Not now, it is not the time for words," says Mama Gambo.

Jasmin smiles through her tears. She hastens to join the workers on their way to Central District and thinks of Mama Gambo. The older woman has seen death. Much death, way before the sickness that took men. Mama Gambo is a monument of pain and suffering.

The death she has seen is of the worst kind.

4

It hurt so much.

That's the opening line of a story that began Mama Gambo's suffering. The opening character is not Mama Gambo—it's the queen. Here is how her story goes:

A bone in the queen's body broke each time the baby flapped, each time its head pushed downward, such was her discomfort. On top of the pangs in her womb, the convulsions in her muscles, the cutting pain in her bones, agony was everywhere: in the stomach, in the groin, in the back. The queen retched every minute and complained about light in the room.

The midwife sealed windows as the mother-to-be started hallucinating, weeping about boulders traveling down her legs, about constant sawing everywhere into her body, about burning, burning, flames in her hips. And the blood! There was so much blood, the floor swam with it.

When, finally, the child quavered into the world, it was coated in a mud of mucus and urine, excrement and blood. Only then, after wiping off sludge, did the midwife realize it wasn't the head that was pushing. It was his feet. Each foot was shaped in a club, not a single toe in sight. The child was also hurting.

It hurt so bad from the poking and prodding, the squeezing and howling, the fevers and chills, he came out skinless but clawed. And there, squirming and heaving, making sounds that were nowhere near an apology for the agony he had caused his mother, just indignation at what he'd suffered, lay what people might expect of a garish creature that had absorbed a hostility of faces, bodies and smells, that had sucked its mother's torment.

And that child was young Prince Magu.

Unsurprising, his mother didn't make it—who would have? It was unthinkable, kind as he was, that the gentle king would alone raise the child that had murdered its mother by simply being born—hence Queen Sheeba.

But the new queen couldn't calm the prince, a weakling that never recovered. It cried and writhed, was fussy about eating. People expected the tot to die any instant—until the day a sorcerer named Atari walked unbidden from a stone at the edge of Mafinga and straight into the palace.

At the edge of Mafinga stood a red-rock monolith, a holy place believed to be an abode of the gods. It was there that the dead were sanctified before they were buried. It was the place where the forefathers lived. From out of this rock, anyone would swear, the stranger Atari had squeezed naked into Mafinga. The sight of him was as drowning as bad breath. He didn't resemble anything they had seen, not with that translucent skin that shifted color as he walked. Everything about him was foreign: a leviathan head on a child's body, big bones pushing against all skin as if he bore a bone sickness.

Atari's hands clasped nothing. He had no herbs or potions. Yet nobody resisted or complained when, wordless, he relieved the queen of the suffering boy. To everyone's astonishment, the child quieted, sucked the stranger's finger and fell asleep in the alien's arms. Whatever it was, no herbs smeared, no potions drank, no chants heeded, Atari's secret magic calmed the boy. Thus, it was—remember the story of Rasputin and his influence over the Romanovs?—Atari became more and more needed, first in the king's palace, then in the entire realm.

Not only was Atari's sorcery altering the young prince and his health, it was also shifting King Chaka. As the prince grew stronger, his clubs uncurling into feet with toes that still needed a stick to walk, the king grew weaker. King Chaka became more recluse. He resigned himself from matters of ruling, made major announcements—the whole Ujamaa affair—through Atari. Even the prince was a shadow to Atari, as was the boy's stepmother, Queen Sheeba.

People whispered about the royals, formed their opinions, but knew nothing of substance. For all they saw was neither King Chaka, Queen Sheeba nor Prince Magu. All they saw was Atari.

He had all the king's blessing and none of his kindness. And, same as how the cockroach that wants to rule over the chicken hires the pale fox as a bodyguard, Prince Magu, now King Magu, found his guardian.

At first people were delighted when the new king showed himself in public, through a screen. This is how he delivered his first speech. By his side stood Atari—his golem form, leviathan head and jutting bones— present as a fart. On the young king's other side was Queen Sheeba, in a flowing gown blooming with flame lilies and wearing a cascading-heart tiara. She sat stern-faced but willing as air to forget her husband's death. Behind them were guards you could count on one hand, but they were effective. Their superior lasers and tasers and jungle camouflage reinforced the king's authority.

King Magu loomed large on-screen. He was dressed in the traditional cloaking of a monarch: leopard skin around his neck, feathers from the plumes of an ostrich on his head. He opened his mouth and the voice that had once belonged to a meerkat was now lowered in octave to boom, transformed, from the speakers:

"Together we are. Mafinga is equal, her people are free. We're good for each other, and we'll work as a unit to eradicate poverty. Individuality is barbaric, so we'll live together. The size of every person's effort will be the measure of the fullness of their stomach. I declare Ujamaa—together we are."

People clapped but they were nonplussed, unclear as to what it all meant. Perhaps a few began to understand as earthmovers rolled and crushed their houses, flattening out space from which would spring Central District with its Ujamaa factory, hospital, school and tech. People found themselves bundled to a compulsory village built of temporary units that could be shipping containers, but temporary became permanent.

And it was only a beginning—things got worse. People had left their homes with the clothes on their backs, clasping nothing but the hands of their children. Anything left behind, including jewelry, was confiscated as property of the state.

Because, in Ujamaa, everyone was equal.

But some were more equal than others. As bulldozers flattened people's houses, plowed up Ujamaas in their stead, further up, excavators cut from the ground a house on a hill fit for a king. Everyone was too stunned to question what happened to "we are community," "the individual is not supreme," "eradicate poverty." Removed from the king's own luxury, people saw poverty—and it was both personal and communal—in manifold.

The transformation of Mafinga happened seemingly overnight. People became their own labor, coerced into the spirit of Ujamaa. Mafinga's departments of Infrastructure, Tourism, Sustainability, Cities, Labor . . . evaporated. Foreign policy became the face of Atari, the golem that had climbed out of a stone.

What was shocking was how worse life developed in Mafinga. Labor-earned food vouchers overturned the currency of the mafinite—a precious stone still harvested but now rare. It was illegal to be in possession of the gemstone, a stone dull as a burp but, on polish, dazzled more than a Betelgeuse star. The wealthy including Baba Gambo were the worst hit.

* * *

Baba Gambo worked at what was once Air Services. He was the lead scientist in major projects on Mafinga's remotely piloted aircrafts. No wonder he could afford the complexity that was his home, a multiroomed sculptural obscenity floating in Parkside. Its roof was giant enough to land flying horses.

The mansion was wrought iron gated, boasting half a dozen bathrooms and yellow-lit windows, most floor to ceiling. A mile-long driveway cut all the way through a lushly grassed garden spilling with hydrangeas, wildfire petals all coral, pink geranium and blue angels. You arrived at a fountain of a curly-haired peeing boy. The twinkling waters of an S-shaped sapphire swimming pool beckoned you to climb in. You resisted and reached an African carved door embossed with stick people, lizards, suns, moons and gods, where, if you used the banger or the bell, a maid would greet you with iced tea infused with honey.

But even that, Baba Gambo's manor house, was bulldozed. Who could blame a man who had built so much and lost everything for not enduring in silence, despite his wife's pleadings?

"You're no better than a madman if you beat the drum for him to dance," she told him. "Only a fool tests the depths of a river with two giant feet," she said.

Did Baba Gambo listen? No. He became the king's most bitter critic. And someone noticed. It was Atari who could and did blame him.

It didn't take much thinking to understand that the new King Magu, heavily in the sorcerer's wing, was nothing close to his father. And like the people of Mafinga, King Magu was decidedly superstitious.

5

Jasmin is pensive.

A philosopher named Mandoza, in his book *Unparalleled*, about the human mind, talks about superstition. It crawls out one by one, a tricreatured beast from a cavern, he says. It stacks its omen against anticipated fears that evolve into disruptions and discontinuities. Superstition makes grown-ups act like children, staring naked and swerving side to side as they try to figure out the uncanny that's the new-found normal. In stupor they reach the place where a transforming lycanthrope or basilisk opens each of its mouths to say in hissing echoes: "Come. With. Me. Now." Superstition, according to Mandoza, is a nonstory that's also a multi-generational delusion even exorcism will not break.

But in the world of Mafinga, full of defeated people, exorcism is not necessary. When King Magu chooses to make an example of someone, who can forget? If a fable of writers drafted a literary canon on the worst of dictators, there might be a pattern in the body of books that make it to the shortlist of a horror award: simple folk swinging . . . birds pecking live eyes . . . burnings, flayings, devourings . . . human skin pink as salmon breasts. But the parable of King Magu will exceed them all. In his record is a list of atrocities, but one stands utmost. And not many remember that the mind and hands behind the atrocity belong to Atari.

It's one thing to enforce attendance to a public execution. Who wants to hear the last cries and gasps of closing eyes? But a crushing? The sorcerer Atari with his monster head and misshapen bones oversaw the execution.

At first the crowd was curious. Nobody knew how the machine shaped like a human worked. When guards put defiant Baba Gambo into it, his cries told them. The king's guards fitted the condemned person into the machine. Then it pulped the person limb by limb. The pulping started in Baba Gambo's hands. You don't want to hear again that sound from a grown man. Not that there are more men left in Mafinga, except for King Magu and his sorcerer Atari. Baba Gambo went silent after the right leg was done.

What spawned out of the machine and into each limb's trough was a heavy mush that looked but didn't smell anywhere near ripe cocoplum fruit.

"Nout a single droup," cried Atari shrilly in his foreign tone.

Citizens watched in revulsion as guards carefully carted away the liquefied remains.

"It's for the king," someone whispered.

"Nonsense."

"How does the king need it?" someone asked.

"The sorcerer's spell keeps King Magu from getting sick. It's a spell that must be fed by human flesh."

"Rubbish."

Someone vomited, and it wasn't Jasmin or Mama Gambo.

A machine dispensed to the dispersing crowd minichocolatox— white and brown six-cubers that dissolved in the mouth, smelled sweeter than milk from the gods and tasted of nothing anyone remembered.

A screen overhead replayed the king's monotone speech: "We will act swiftly and resolutely to eradicate revolutionaries who seek to pervade Mafinga with the poison of individualistic thinking. Our duty is to contribute to the whole, not to diminish it with selfish thought."

The pulp machine did one more job on another dissenter as the sundial cast its shadow on Mafinga. By then the citizens understood the language of a lunatic.

Whether it was a personal vendetta or the greatest scare of all time, it worked. Baba Gambo's crime? He said to a socialist state: "You stole everything. But I'm a thinker and everything I need is in my head."

Atari crushed the head.

So you see. The death Mama Gambo has witnessed is of the worst kind. How does she do it? wonders Jasmin. How does she get up night by night, and will the composure to go on?

6

Light grows as you near Central District.

Out yonder, a neon sign against the face of Ujamaa Factory says: *A philosophy of the people.*

Pzzz. An overhead screen blares with the melodic chant of a cartoon. Teenagers in white T-shirts and flowing bloomers perform athletic drills to a *toot!* guided by a woman in combat fatigues. Inside the ad, able-bodied girls sprint along hand-drawn lanes and whistle over hurdles. *Toot!* Flexed arms pull back and spear javelins into the horizon. *Toot!* Sparring athletes dance around each other in elaborate footwork and wrestle in earnest, inside sandpits.

Happiness is the story of us, says the neon sign.

As teens test out team virtue in tug o' wars, cast giant shotputs into the air that *smash!* into the ground, the humans marching—too many of them out in the cold—pound to an insignificant beat.

Unsafe in the streets, citizens pass surveillance. Headless eyes up high, unseen to the human gaze, swivel in automation. Cameras follow each body, roving sights on the rib of a wall, the ear of a roof. Sometimes scrutiny is in the watch of a neighbor who needs no shuttle spacer or chopper with guards to pick at clues, to loiter their gossip as if it were wildflowers frantic for self-worth.

Jasmin remembers flowers. Memories of them come and go. She thinks of impala lilies, their vibrant blooms in clusters of pink and white. She pulls out facts from the recesses of her mind. The impala lily can be sweet-smelling or carrion-smelling—depends on luck, or what you're made of. The impala lily grows taller than a man. Her deciduous succulence is unassuming in the first half of the year. In July, sometimes September, her flowers and leaves start to bloom, first in scatter, then in cluster. A deadly woman, she's useful for hunting. If she chooses, she spits toxic water, the anatomy of arrow poison. The shudder that reaches its victim is a shadow, black as ink. It hides nothing in its travel through the bloodstream, incapacitates if you're lucky. But often it's death by default. Proteas are kinder. They are gods of shape, soft in hue. As for the deep yellow daisies, long and blooming, they are nothing like the people of Mafinga, once thriving but must now watch life go by.

Jasmin imagines Mia and Omar on their way to brainwash. Is Mia, without speaking, trotting as she goes, riding an unseen beast? Does Mama Gambo's caring voice shift in gears, grasp for control, where there is none? For she must do nothing else but deliver the children to Ujamaa Yaya, to the manipulation of others who'll feed them propaganda, coach them to become robots of the state. Jasmin wants to fall on her knees on the gravel, to cry to the gods of the ancestors who have let this happen.

7

Mafinga is a small country, so tiny, you can walk around it in hours if the system lets you. But the system doesn't encourage meander. It guides Jasmin and the rest to Central District.

In Central District people scatter in groups. Everyone understands duty. But it's more than duty. Showing up at Ujamaa Factory, Ujamaa Tech, Ujamaa Medico, Ujamaa Yaya or whatever Ujamaa designated workplace—the Ujamaas evolve all the time—means a roof over your heads, food for your children. No one owns the units they live in. No one goes to a shop with mafinite to buy eggs, milk, flour, sugar, tea. Jasmin remembers with longing these commodities she reads about in the story machine. But her memory is not just from the story machine. She can almost swear she's drank tea, beaten eggs with sugar, butter and vanilla—what a pleasant word—to make a cake. How is it that can she remember and not remember all at once?

She's read stories where protagonists go to a butcher and ask for a tenderloin, rib eye, fillet, chicken breast, lamb chop. She's seen pictures of what market-fresh means: glowing red tomatoes, screaming-yellow lemons, rich green spinach—and that's before you get to the cowfish, rock lobster, tilapia. There are butter sizzles and drizzling pancakes, fragrant toast and chewy sourdough bread, swollen with yeasty pride. Wine that pours in liquid gold full of bubbles into a twinkling flute.

Something happened, because she knows of this other world. It's a knowledge that feels lived, not an immersion of reading. She knows of the world's concepts, its pleasures and philosophies.

But it's a world far-flung from Mafinga where all you get is canned potatolux. You microwave it for your children and eat what's left. The supplements, all capsulated, are there to wash into your stomach with treated water. Jasmin takes them sporadically, not faithfully as the system demands. She doesn't know why she disobeys this requirement. At the back of her mind, she thinks it's something to do with Godi.

UJAMAA

1

Central District is soaked in light that never reduces in glare. Incessant strobes of illumination assault you. It's a relief to enter the factory.

Inside, you see people's faces, settled after they clock-in, after they abandon their coats to the cloaks supervisor who neatly tickets them. The cloakroom is also the main office where they keep books, tally progress, issue vouchers. Everyone except the guards is in a plain tunic or a khaki blouse, formless pants. Clothes are woven inside Ujamaa Textile, issued to each citizen by the state. The factory supervisors wear hi-vis jackets, mostly yellow with silver highlights, but sometimes the jackets are orange. There's a loiter of guards in army fatigues. Even as they feign indifference, the few guards are scouting the workers, picking out discord.

The factory is a large monolithic thing, a ground building rectangular and partitioned in frames. It has conveyor belts and powered machinery. The canteen is a spotless place—space everywhere. Sometimes it serves something hot: boiled rice and beans (never spiced), warmed maize porridge (never honeyed), salted yams (never splashed with ghee). It's as if indulging the belly will make workers useless. So mostly it's flat bread (nothing roasted, fried or grilled).

Guards don't interact with workers, unless they must, where "interact" is a synonym for "lethal force." Generally, they sentry the factory and its doors. There's Maridadi—she's tall, shaped how a woman should be: curves in the right places. Her long, slippery hair falls to her hips. She's voluptuous even in fatigues. Her fingers are lightly rested on the taser gun in her belt. She pretends she's not looking, but everyone knows she's got tabs on poor Violet, pebbles in her head. The worker is rocking herself and muttering: "Inside TV. Contained in the system. Eyes everywhere. No redemption." Violet wears the kind of darkness you'd mistake for purple, the flower's hue. But so gaunt, she's all skin and eyes, and always muttering things people dare not say out loud.

Jasmin's worker card says she's thirty-six years old. She doesn't remember much of those years, and nothing before Omar was born. How did she lose her years, or soar to new time? She wonders about the others, what they remember. Citizens no longer look stunned as they were in those first days of the sickness, as fathers, brothers, husbands, sons started dropping in droves overcome by blisters and heatwave. Godi got sick. Jasmin looks at the women, wonders if she's become them—wearing a face that says she survives, only just.

Sometimes you can tell the ones who find escape in books from hidden story machines, readers who try not to get caught. Like old woman Apiyo and the pale glows she insists were once chestnut eyes. Her nose is flat but, if you look closely, it is strong with the smell of hope. Her kinky hair is long and tangled, full of silver that won't buy her freedom. But the sag of her cheeks tells of many tears, some shed for her sons Abebe and Baako, who perished with the sickness.

"How can we keep this up," says Jasmin.

"As we always have," says Mama Apiyo. "We're citizens of habit. Look not where you stand, but where you last slipped. This is how you survive."

Toot! The whistle.

"Quiet already!" It's Thrifty the supervisor. The big-voiced hairy one. "This group here. Corridor side. You lot there. Conveyor belt—fittings."

The *You lot there* comprises Jasmin, Apiyo, J and Bake.

"What about the cold?" asks Bake out loud.

"I want to see some moving," snaps Thrifty.

"But it's cold."

"Smother the complaints."

"What's with the heater?" says Bake.

"Creature comforts is all. Now. Move!"

Like guards, supervisors are the king's puppets, faithful to deliver justice, entrusted with more freedom so they can keep order. Tonight, control is elusive. Everyone's on edge.

"What's with the fittings?" says J. She's always angry, her pock-marked face making her look more cross. "Who knows what these things even *do*?"

"You're lucky Thrifty can't hear you," says Blue, the pacifier. Charcoal black skin, white, white teeth. "It's the king's command. You just do it."

"Some sort of start, you have to admit," says Jasmin.

"You mean the silent lights—what happened to the reader?" says Ten.

"Stop fishing to know who knows what," says Jasmin. She doesn't trust Ten. How do you trust someone with a head full of dandruff and peeling cornrows?

"And who said it was a reader?" asks Bake. "For all we know . . ."

Toot! The whistle. "I want to see the conveyor belt moving. Speed it, girls! No stoppages."

"One more word and I'll fist her," mutters J.

"What's that?" Thrifty is approaching. She's flicking her baton. Her face pushes into J's. "You have special comments?"

"It's nothing." Old woman Apiyo eases the supervisor gently away. "We have much to get through. No?" There's wisdom behind her sidewise glance to the girls. Get moving. Even J obeys. You obey someone with that many folds on her neck.

They labor silently. Fitting after fitting of who knows what. It's the king's command. Each shiny thing is designed to screw into something else—perhaps a giant machine that must have a purpose. What if they are creating another pulp machine?

A wash of music makes them forget the questions. Like the ones Jasmin wants to ask about her lover, Solo. Music guides their activity and goes choppy when it wants them to work faster, harder. Soulful when it wants to imbue them with a false sense of amity, like now at snack time. The flat bread is tough, barely flavored with salt. A flute plays as Jasmin takes another bite.

"Hey you." It's Hotel, the other supervisor. The generous one with her albino blondes: pale hair, pale brows.

"Hey," says Jasmin.

"Holding up good?"

"I suppose."

"Solo?"

"Haven't seen her in three months." Sometimes Jasmin's not sure Solo was even there. She doesn't remember—the details so hazy. But the mafinite squirreled in her unit tells her Solo's visit wasn't a dream. "What's going on in the mines?"

"I'll find out for you."

"Thanks, Hotel."

"It's all good."

"Really. Thank you."

Toot!

"Better—"

"That would be right," agrees Hotel. She nods at Thrifty in the distance with her baton. "Stay away from that one."

Jasmin and the rest labor silently. Fitting after fitting until just before dawn.

Toot!

It's the end-of-shift file for rations that supervisors hand out. Laminated food vouchers, ticket-sized, and baby jars of vitamin supplements.

Hotel slips Jasmin a bar of soap. As Jasmin turns, she hears: "Hey you!"

Her heart stops.

2

It's Maridadi. Her fingers are no longer on the taser in her belt. They are pointing at Jasmin.

"You! Stop right there!"

The voice is a bullet. It doesn't stop Jasmin. She quickens her pace. Now she's elbowing, pushing past workers. She's searching for a space in the crowd, a place to blend in. The soap is a burn in her pocket.

"Stop right now!"

Jasmin takes to disoriented running, but it's hard to run in a crowd. Some of them are turning, a murmur of voices. Jasmin throws a panicked look back. She sees Hotel, shaking her head. Jasmin doesn't understand, she must get away. But the crowd is pushing back, trampling away from the exit, forcing her back to Maridadi, who is standing legs akimbo, and pointing at Jasmin.

"You disgust me."

Blackness washes over Jasmin. Inside her nausea, she hears the mutters. "Inside TV. Contained in the system. Eyes everywhere. No redemption."

She looks up. Maridadi is not pointing at Jasmin. Her focus is on Violet who's standing next to Jasmin. The woman's eyes are shining. Her mutter is climbing into a chant. Words tumble out of Violet's mouth. "Inside TV. Contained in the system. Eyes everywhere. No redemption. Inside TV. Contained in the system. Eyes everywhere. No redemption!"

Maridadi is approaching. She's walking fast, her taser drawn. "I said stop it." Her sound and words are out of sync. Her smile—she's relishing commotion, a chance for correction.

"No redemption! No redemption!"

Maridadi is running. She and the taser part the crowd as Moses did with his rod in the story of the exodus, when a whole sea parted.

Violet's face is lit. Her eyes are wide. She swings, but her palm connects with nothing. It's as if she's warding off demons. "No redempthum!" Her words are losing coherence. "Redempthum." Her mouth is distorted, drool sliming down.

"Redemp—"

Maridadi launches with a roar. Her strike cuts Violet's chant. The guard doesn't pull the trigger to discharge electricity. She leaps and whacks Violet on the head with the weapon.

Violet crumples to the cemented floor. The crowd is silent.

"Redemp-thum. Red-emp-thum."

Maridadi's assault is committed. There's a gasp, from Violet or the crowd. Maridadi presses with her knees on the fallen worker, and rams her again with force on the head.

J begins forward, her fists balled.

Mama Apiyo grabs J. "Don't." Her whisper scratches. "It's suicide. You know this." J struggles, but Mama Apiyo holds.

Now J is crying against the older woman.

Violet's convulsing, hands and legs jerking.

There's blood everywhere. Blood and bones. The hitting is now a sickly crunch. Obscene. Violet moves, a twitch. She goes still.

Ten begins laughing. It's a hysterical laughter. Jasmin doesn't know where the slap comes from. But it's effective and rings in her hand. It silences Ten.

Violet's head is a mural on the floor.

"What are you staring at?" says Maridadi. She's soft spoken, coos her words as if they're a lullaby. "Then what?" She stands tall on the fluid-soaked floor.

"Go!" It's Hotel. She's pushing the factory workers toward the exit. "I said go!"

Her words spark the immobilized mob. Now nobody is waiting, but their leaving is not in a hurry. They brood out into the departing night. The glare of Central District will gradually dim until it dies somewhere along the way to Ujamaa Village.

Jasmin's tunic is a splash artist's canvas. It's coated with pieces of Violet.

3

Stick a knife in the heart and turn it twice. Hers is a world of hurt. The stretch to Ujamaa Village is today a long way out. The road is choked with bunched-up people who speak sparingly, or not at all. Who can blame them after what they've seen?

Jasmin wants to fold into herself, but she must stay strong for Mia and Omar. She remembers a microfiction from the story machine. A crime tale by an author named Temper. It's about a widow in bleakness who swears to stay strong for the children. Each morning she wakes with a prayer. "I must stay strong for the children."

One day her words shift, an earthquake of moving words, loosening rocks pressed into all sides of her. "I must stay strong from the children. From the children." Over and over. The children's play is a deafening sound. Is that a laugh, a flute or a wail? The widow can't remember. The sound is bruising.

The words are first raised bumps on her skin, but soon they are giant blotches. She shivers from the welts, the children's laughter burning, burning. She rushes out of the house. A taxi is waiting. "St. Judes," she cries. "Take me now to St. Judes." The church is packed but feels empty. Its pews stay cold, no matter how long the widow sits on the same spot. A preacher is jumping at the pulpit, but the sermon isn't grounding. Not for the widow, it isn't.

All she hears is something abstract on the mind of Christ, on the wisdom of the world—or a lack thereof. Something about finding truth in the character of God, who is a woman, and she's lent her son to nails, bloody nails, tearing into flesh on a cross. The widow staggers to her feet, crawls and falls out of the church, as behind the pastor shrieks: "Stick a spike in the heart, turn it, turn it."

A taxi is waiting, no doors opening—just a black tomb that crawls into the widow's stomach and stays. Who can blame what the widow does next? As the story unfolds, there's more to the tale. The whodunit is not the widow or the taxi driver, but the church. Insatiable in her yearning for communal sacrifice.

Vengeance is how Jasmin feels.

A mist rises on the horizon. Soon it will be light. The crowd walks fast to best the approaching dawn. It begins pouring. A gray heavy rain that washes away bits of Violet strewn on Jasmin. She detaches with the mothers from the rest of them. They are not many, mothers.

They slip into Mama Gambo's unit for a collection.

Sometimes Mama Gambo greets them with the children at the door. Today, with the rain, she's inside. It's not like the unit is spilling with progeny. Any child from ten goes to the factory, but even those now are scarce. You can count them on just about two hands. Mafinga's future is in peril. The system's propaganda has snatched promising little ones, and you get to see them on-screen, singing slogans. It seems ages since they were taken, some as infants. Their mothers have long forgotten them.

The remaining ones—including Mia and Omar, eleven of them—are no more than Mia's age for the littlest. But they look the same, miniature—the kind of frame you get from malnourish. Even nine-year-old Joko, he stands, a guard, a pretend rifle in his hand. He's barely an inch taller than Omar. Joko will use whatever he gets to soldier and point at people, pull a trigger. Now it's a stick, a broom, a brush . . . His mother Kijiji beats him, but he won't stop doing it.

There are the Moyo twins, Hope and Art, unidentical. Their mother Apunda—it means one who is beside herself—has pock-marked skin and used to wear a dangle of bead necklaces before

Ujamaa, the "everyone is equal" ideology. The girl, Hope, has big, black eyes, plaits in her brown hair. She's silent as a basenji—it's a hunting dog. Her brother Art's head is always razor-shaven, an obsession. He's always arranging things, including the children. He demands where they sit, how they sit, stand, play . . . even though they don't really play. The children have no inkling of what fun might constitute.

There are the Triba triplets, birthed late. Their mother Matatizo is sad as a warthog and just as belligerent if you cross her wrong. You have Imani, flat-nosed, a gap in his tooth. Despite his shortness, he's solid as a hammer. Potbellied Lia, meek as a rabbit, her face full of mourning. Every time you see her, she's minutes from a cry. Her other brother Sabre is all teeth, an overgrown bite easily fixed but unattended.

Mama Gambo's hut is simple, like the rest in Ujamaa Village. The brainwashed children are contained, none rushing and falling into their mothers. They are stripped of excitement, conditioned to restraint. Everyone except Mia is on the floor, neat in a corner, knees up and clasped in their hands. They wait, patient, until their mothers call them and each will dutifully stand and offer a hand for gripping. But Omar finds her legs, presses into Jasmin's body.

"Mia is sleeping," he says. He points at Mama Gambo's mattress.

Suddenly it's all too much for Jasmin.

"Are you crying?" asks Omar.

She shakes her head but is unable to stop the tears. Her mind's vision is lucid with Maridadi's hourglass frame flying into Violet. Pieces of Violet everywhere.

Mama Gambo waits until everyone has dispersed. "What's the story?"

"I am lost."

"To be lost is to learn the way. Be your mountain or lean on one. Will you tell me?"

"You won't believe if you haven't seen it."

"Try me—have I not seen worse?"

"The tenseness. It's grim."

"So?"

"The guards are beasts."

"And that's news—how? Or should I ask who?"

"Violet."

Mama Gambo clicks her tongue. "In misfortune we learn wisdom. A child learns by falling." She shakes her head, spits on the ground. She looks over the stains on Jasmin's tunic. "How bad?" She says it as if she already knows the answer.

"Grave."

"Evil has no eyes to choose. The one who uses force is afraid to reason. The stars are not playing well. But it is what it is."

"What does it tell you?"

"That the system is afraid of us." Mama Gambo nods with her chin at Mia, curled into her arms on the floored mattress. "Take these ones home. They are the reward of life. Teach them love, not fear."

She presses something soft and speckled into Jasmin's hand. "For them."

"What—"

"Careful."

Jasmin looks. "Why! It's an egg."

"A little protein will do the children good."

"I stopped the supplements. For me and them."

"Why?"

"Something Godi said before—" she looks away, unable to speak it.

"Dying steals from you."

"I remember it vaguely, what he said. It felt right to stop the supplements."

"Good."

"You know something to tell me?"

"How long is it since you stopped?" asks Mama Gambo.

"A few months maybe. Why?"

"Are memories coming and going?"

"Flashbacks, yes. How do you . . . Maybe I should restart . . ."

"Never. Those things they dish out suppress your mind."

Jasmin stares at Mama Gambo. "And you didn't think to tell me?"

"The things that happen." Mama Gambo's voice changes with the wretchedness of a memory. "Sometimes it's better to forget."

"Yes." Jasmin touches Mama Gambo's arm. "But you haven't. Forgotten."

"I have never taken the supplements."

They stand, a moment, unified in the silence and comfort of human touch. Then Jasmin reaches into her pocket. "It's a little wet."

Mama Gambo puts the soap to her nose. "Goat's milk." She folds it into her pocket. "Get home before the sun comes out."

Mia doesn't rouse as Jasmin scoops her. She's limp, arms dangling, her head on Jasmin's shoulder. Little purrs in her sleep. If Omar notices the stained tunic, still bloodied despite the rain, he says nothing. If he deciphered any of the conversation with Mama Gambo, he's not showing it. But once or twice he looks up at Jasmin's face as they make for her unit where she'll add a splash of water into a bowl of powdered potato and whisk bright yellow yolk into gruel, then she'll wake Mia. She smiles. A good mother knows what her children will eat. And today she's a good mother—she has an egg. For what rubbish is potatolux, other than sustenance for slaves?

Suddenly, Jasmin is so tired. She just wants to take off her bra, to lie cradling her children on her mattress.

4

Her head is full of words she recognizes, the paradox of author Shellon unmoored in her head. Text scrolled in fragmented pockets. Sometimes the language of this text blurts out unbidden. Blackout poetry creeping out of the door, down the bald road and its yawn of empty. There's a sullenness in its step, a questioning: why does the system call up extinction?

For without men, or a nudging to procreate, where will new babies come from? The youngest, about the same age as Mia, mark the timeframe of fate's abolition of men. But the air of absence is not just associated with missing men, as one might expect, but with every woman and child falling into a nonworld that is the system. How is this an existence?

Darkness stalks inwards from the west. And with it, more rain. The roof stays silent. It never leaks noise. Can't be corrugated roofing but looks it. No melodic drumming on the top, the music of a cloudburst, of downpour. Even if there was music, Jasmin can't sing to accompany its notes. In this world there's no song.

Soon the sun will set, bringing with it nightfall. Every night is a ritual. The children abandoned at Mama Gambo's. Groups peeling off at destination—those who go to Ujamaa Medico, Ujamaa Tech . . . Ujamaa Factory is the terminus. Jasmin hopes she can catch sleep in the last wisp of day when the rest of the world is asleep.

Mia is lightly snoring, Omar in his comatose slumber. The world is asleep, but the system is wakeful in propaganda. King Magu is on set with another speech:

"I thank the people of Mafinga—you're free from the burdens of individuality. Selfishness is toxic. The consensus of community demands that . . ."

Now the screen is playing the *Hau, Hau, Acha We* song, its toxin wrapped in a melody from children in sisal skirts and face paint. Their mouths get bigger, swallowing the screen, reaching to consume Jasmin . . . and she bursts to wakefulness.

Her head is pounding. She thinks of the system's barbarity. Maridadi's blows on a caving skull, blows now in her own head. The bang, bang of a migraine. How does one unsee Violet in a river of blood? Hotel put a blanket over the body, but it soaked up the crimson and covering made no difference. You knew who was inside, how damaged.

Jasmin lays quiet in the room, her sleeping children purring on the mattress. It's still light, she knows. But the unit with its automated shutters is wrapped in darkness. Enveloped in the dread of a new night when duty will call, and the children will be shunted off to Ujamaa Yaya. There, teachers tasked to raise the right heads into society will make sure each child is right headed. The system is fiercely succeeding in creating mules, muses Jasmin, bar her own clever little ones. Mia and Omar with the genes of their father and the subversion of their mother who teaches them book knowledge.

On days such as this, she misses Godi. There are stories in her head, tales of his smell, intricate as a star, luminous in this remembering. There are no myths about his scent, its brightness, positioning or direction. Just the scorching dance of its legend at the end of a long, long night. His touch is a perfect constellation, mummified beyond an autumn sky.

He always said, "Two ants will pull a grasshopper."

Dear Godi. She needs him now more than ever to pull away the grasshopper that pervades Mafinga. She misses his wisdom. His empathy. She misses their chemistry. What founds chemistry? Such perplexity. That connection that you get generates yearning or disaffection in its absence. No college, school of thought, enlightenment or self-help opus can teach it. Once you feel it, you become a prisoner of the past. You know when you have it—the evocation of a touch, a kiss that's also a fruit so floral, how fresh, it gives precision to your longing. You know when you lack it—the ordeal of a clench, a twist away, the revulsion of a caress most pungent. It's aged cheese that puckers you up, disagrees with your very being. Nothing but your body knows to give in or push away, to find rapture or rude awakening. The right chemistry, the one she had with Godi, is always consenting. Her body went soft in the empire of his arms. He was metahuman, that's how he felt, his kiss full of wilderness.

Theirs was a sapiosexuality. She was enamored by his intelligence. His handiwork with the now banished story machines. Godi was a solar engineer. Together, they built a home that understood dreams, laughter, stories. He introduced her to the author Maddison who wrote:

> Stories are no daily rundown from a startled artist. They are not extinct wishes conjured from a sea. But a story could be about a stuttering blackbird, its mind full of yolk. The bird could be the epitome of an imbecile monarch. The story could lift and descend in a mood. It could tell you about thumbprints on absent paper cut from an oblivious tree. Such calamity it would have been had Sylvia Pathos listened to old brays of the heart but never written a single let alone final word!

Godi introduced Jasmin to other silver liners: Shellon. Harper. Mandoza. Gladwell . . . Writers whose language gave promise, adorned courage, unearthed identity, grabbed freedom. Their words were silver bullets, immutable vests.

5

The house full of stories that she built with Godi was no exclusive park-side indulgence of tailor-made kitchens, exquisite finishes. It was a simple three-bed. A single-storied log house with a sloping roof. Simple, but home. And home is where the heart is.

His death was more than heartbreak. It was disenchantment. How dare he? She closed her heart, never minding the enslavement such closure promised. Happy never after—his dying breached her belief. What was that about it was all in the stars? Betelgeuse couldn't save him. It was never in the stars.

Unable to sleep, she leaves the children scattered on the mattress. Mia, nearest to her, has a hand carelessly thrown across her brother's face. Jasmin arranges the children to neatness. She listens to Mia's purring, observes Omar's sleep like death, and she's certain they're goners in slumber.

She unsheathes the story machine from its hiding place underneath the microwave. She wears the headphones, glides to the floor, her back to the wall. The sun, so deadly, so useful. She smiles wryly, wonders how many more of Godi's solar-powered machines full of stories are out there in the world, subverting minds.

She switches the machine to audio, to the caressing voice of Shellon—who knows to tell a story in all its verse, bridge, refrain, elision and outro. This new story named 'Whimsical' is about a woman on the morning after her unconsummated wedding night.

She wanders, uncertain, and finds a black oak tree in the forestland just outside her new husband's home. Her heart flutter tells her of an instant swooning—she's smitten. The oak tree is everything she imagined. He's tens of feet tall, absorbs her affection as she rubs against him, moans into his smelly wood.

Each evening after supper she flees her baffled husband, to grind against her lover's giant body, his grooved trunk all gray and three feet wide. One moonless night it's all black, and memory and her nose for the tree's yeasty scent guide her to him.

One day her husband steals in her trail, finds her pressed to the hardwood, her face and arms caressing the oak. The spouse rears back astonished, then recovers and shouts in a messy way: "It's not even mahogany or teak!"

The husband's jealousy knows no bounds, and the giant creature winds up felled, shaped and polished into a chiffonier. He is smaller and more delicate, his chest decorated with drawers, his crown gilded with an antique mirror that sparkles when the chandelier is lit. Right there in her bedroom, the lovers realize they're closer than ever. She strokes him at whim, at the last possible moment, day or night.

But the husband's fury reduces the chiffonier to hard wood, scattered onto a rubbish pile. A waste collector astute for treasure secures the timber, nails it to the shape of a park bench, sells it at a palm-off price to the local council. Now you see the woman, at the story's climax, night after night, divorced but blissful. She is sprawled on her lover's long-dead seat, arms around his backrest, her longing for all eight hundred years of him intact.

Jasmin longs for Godi like this, despite the system and its selfishness or jealousy. She steps back into the mattress and squeezes beside her children. She closes her eyes, and the surrealism of forbidden text comforts her mind.

6

Wednesday.

Doors open, doors close. Like the automated window shutters that rise and fall on a timer, everything acts on system whim. You don't need to draw the curtains or flush the toilet. You don't touch anything—the system controls everything. It tells you what to eat, what to wear. Potatolux churned and canned at Ujamaa Factory is good for you. Underwear designed and sewn at Ujamaa Factory is good for you—now it rubs intimately against Jasmin's skin. Boots the system owns are good for you. With the food and uniform's calibrated fit, there's nothing to distract Jasmin from duty. The system goads from distraction, controls more than wear and touch. It infiltrates memory.

Jasmin wonders whether she should share her knowledge with the women at the factory. But Mama Gambo's words last night when Jasmin asked about it reverberate in her head:

"It's foolishness to speak it to anyone."

"But why?" asked Jasmin.

"The heart of the wise woman lies quiet."

"But words may be the only foolishness we can afford," said Jasmin. "Shouldn't we look out for each other? You know as well as I do that the system doesn't care an inch about us."

Mama Gambo touched her arm. "Will you fight when you're

carrying a basket full of eggs?" She nodded at Mia and Omar. "These children are your eggs. Never compromise them."

"It just appears that you've forgotten we have no husbands, Mama Gambo. We're all relatives of each other. There are workers in the factory—the Mama Apiyos and the Violets—who are close as family. And without family I am poor."

"Yes, we have no husbands. Atari thought that killing my husband was burying a library. But don't you see? He only released the text. Now it is many, and we must be wise with it."

"I didn't mean it that way . . . Baba Gambo . . ."

Mama Gambo shook her head firmly. "You can't unwind your words. If your only tool is a hammer, you'll treat everything as a nail. Much is wasted on useless words. All I am saying is the night has ears." She nodded at Omar, pretending not to listen, at Mia, purring in her sleep. "For them, remember. Always for them. They are our legacy."

"Is there anyone I can trust?"

"In Mafinga? No."

"Not even you?"

"Especially me."

It was then that Jasmin understood. She suddenly knew how Mama Gambo did it, how she woke up night by night, took other people's children despite her own pain. Hers was an inside bellow. And the cow that bellows does so for all the cows.

Baba Gambo's death was not in vain.

* * *

So, Jasmin can't tell the others at the factory that the supplements enforce order, diffuse intelligence. That they make real memory go and fill you with ideas of what the dead husbands looked like, smelled like.

But Jasmin remembers Godi's smell. He smelled of old books: a sweet smell of vanilla and almonds. She thinks this in the monotony of the night. Every night in the factory is monotonous. Now she's making fittings for incongruous machines whose purpose she might never see. Now it's lids, tin after tin of potatolux ticking to a timer down the conveyor belt. Now it's bland liquid soap in squeezable jars for Ujamaa Facility.

Clatter-clatter-clatter. The factory makes huge noise. It's a clock, all parts synchronous. The guards, the supervisors—they are its face, its arms, its dials and displays. You see a guard, a supervisor, and you amp up your effort. *Ticky-tock-tock* hums the clock. You slave the night away. The workers are the wheels. They work lever by lever, back and forth, back, forth. *Zip-papa, zip-papa*, hums the machine. The conveyor belt moves. Further down, a different machine goes *wroom-wroom*, cogs and all. Amalgamated, the factory roars, hums, titters its sounds full of notes and phrases. It plays down the silent rebellion of potential dissenters like Apiyo, the old woman, whose chorus of disapproval takes the form of compliance.

It's Apiyo's amenableness that keeps the rest of the women alive, even as they step gingerly along the unsoiled floor, none of the previous night's bloodshed visible. They listen to Apiyo's quiet leadership, even as the factory goads them with its sounds.

Clatter-clatter-clatter. Ticky-tock-tock. Zip-papa, zip-papa. Wroom-wroom.

7

Monitors everywhere in silent display. Dark telescopic eyes high on poles, swiveling on cameras. Big black speakers—there's always music or an announcement, when a guard or supervisor is not blowing a whistle.

Announcements broadcast as they do in the high street on the road to Central District. Neon lights glow red-orange above a screen that shouts phrases:

"Our collective good."

"Others value you for what you do, not what you get."

The response of the living dissolves behind shuttered windows. The workers wear like bandannas their guilt for existing. Their self-esteem is deceased. It stalks, a zombie tramp, groaning and bleating a ritual of dying in the incongruous melting of an unbalanced world whose storm does not choose where it strikes. Yet the sky halos a palace where nothing happened for years, then the king begot a rat and a stranger climbed from a rock.

Music without lyrics seeps from the speakers.

The oppressor comes with music that steals into your soul, snatches your wings. Classical music with its strings and woodwinds, percussion and brass. Its homophonic melody leaves you patterned with scars of forgetting. As the bassoon rises and fades in warm vibrations of precision layered with mastery, you disremember choice, mindfulness and space. You forget simple pleasures like walking the dog in a bath of sunlight. Licking ice cream from a caramel-dipped cone. Skipping barefoot along a white-sanded beach. The tune bemoans dead loves and lovers in an airy float, but you're stuck in grit and toil where the little you have is privilege, and the rest is earned.

But Jasmin disallows the music to brainwash her. She thinks about the philosopher Mandoza who wrote about tyranny in his book titled *Narrowness*, scribbled in a prison cell that transformed him. He wrote:

> The oppressor comes with flowers that pull you apart from family and draw you to strobing gravity that is a scratchless itch in every pore. The flowers are winter blooms that are never white or pink, purple or blue-tinted. As you imagine a shape-shifting god in the vibrant iris of your mind, the impala lilies and proteas, daisies and violets fade into nothing. You are overwhelmed by words like "wrong" or "impossible," "basic" or "unfussy," and phrases like "social order" or "greater good" that take control of your destiny until, the guinea pig you are, you forget about the flowers and the music, and any hope of flight or dreams.

She remembers how, like an animal in a cell, in some remote island hidden in a bay, the author Mandoza who became a president understood with such clarity the oppressor. The sort of questions he asked wove shame into his captors inside the borders of a country that had forgotten its aura. It was easier to look away, to flee and not look back and turn to salt, than wait for a cock's third crow. The country slept through sunlight, gale and thunderstorm, pressed its paw to some lugubrious vision, as cigarettes and bullets did the talking.

Mafinga has no cigarettes, but bullets have morphed into tasers and lasers. It has oppressors in the king, his sorcerer and his guards, his supervisors, the system and the sun. What good comes from a climate that takes men at their peak? All the able-bodied dead, torn skin by skin by a deadly cancer that first bruised, then speckled them with lesions that carpeted the body, before breaking it into furrows that fell away or leaked.

Even children know: whatever happens, beware the sun. They know to keep themselves tucked away or sleeping by day. One never forgets—the little remembering you have worries you out of forgetting the afflicted who became the dead. And through this torment or containment by fear, supplements condition you to sleep.

The one man untainted by disease was a closeted Elvis, studded jumpsuits in his cupboard. Him, the guards took. They dragged him to a center court, debrained him with a bullet.

8

Clatter-clatter-clatter. Zip-papa, zip-papa. Wroom-wroom.

"Jasmin."

She looks up. "Yes?"

It's Ten. Her breath is a henhouse. She has scaly patches on her head, a furious scalp. Her dandruff condition is today worse. She's scratching flakes of yellow scales the size of fingernails.

"I just—" Still scratching, and it's shitting Jasmin. "I got something to show you."

"I can't now. You know that."

"But you must! Come, please."

"And who will look after the machine?"

Clatter-clatter-clatter.

Ten points. Blue is approaching.

"Shifts are shifts," says Jasmin. Only sickness or a death disrupts a shift. "Maridadi—"

"Maridadi knows. Just come, please." Ten's scratching spreads the scales from her head to the spotless floor.

"Easy with those things. Try vinegar from Ujamaa Canteen. Ulafi will demand a spleen—it's better than scalping yourself."

Ulafi runs Ujamaa Canteen. It's tucked in a row, one of the units at Ujamaa Village. When its side wall lifts, Ulafi pops out her head and rips off people. She's in the system's pocket. Nothing she sells the system does not control. What she sells is nothing lavish—basic things: raw nuts, brown rice, powdered greens, condensed milk. Practical things: night socks, needles and threads, sanitary pads . . . Sometimes, at an unfair trade, she palms you a rare treat: scented soap, unpackaged. Food vouchers, small value. Boiled sweets, nothing of the kind Jasmin remembers: Peanut brittles. Pear drops. Aniseed balls. Acid drops. Black bullets. Fruit rocks. Rhubarb twists. Custard mushies. Lemon fizz. Pineapple cubes. Sweet monkey nuts. The treats Ulafi sells—she's a shrewd little thing with a lust for profit—are folded and hard all the way, made in copper pots, no flavoring.

How much would a few drops of vinegar to ease Ten's dandruff cost?

Ten is still frantic, vigorous as she nails out scales.

"Scraping makes it worse," says Jasmin.

"It just feels . . ."

Jasmin shakes her head. "Maybe I'll follow if you stop scratching."

"Okay."

"Whatever it is you're planning, it smells trouble. And I can't afford trouble. Neither can you."

Ten shrugs.

Jasmin follows, self-conscious. Camera eyes are watching. Factory eyes everywhere. Cameras in cylindrical vents overhead, the color of foil. Jasmin looks around. There is Bake, doing potatolux tins with J. Bake waves. Jasmin waves back. J stays sullen, her pockmarked face dancing in the lights. Mama Apiyo is nowhere. Sometimes, because of her age, they put her on special duty: canteen—packing crackers for the workers' snack time; main office—laminating food vouchers; packaging—restocking jars of vitamin supplements.

Jasmin treads after Ten, creeping along corridors past the plant room. No sign of Thrifty and her boom voice. Hotel is preoccupied in the east wing where they are soling boot after boot, handcrafted. The factory mirrors the outdoors. On hot nights it's blistery. On wintry nights, you know the rest. Today it's balmy.

Jasmin is astonished to arrive at the toilet and its stone-white tiles. "What?" she blurts, goes silent at a bowl's gurgle as someone flushes in a cubicle. She's staggered to see who swoops out of it: Maridadi, immaculate in newly pressed fatigues. Jasmin's heart flutters, but there's nowhere to go.

Maridadi's glance doesn't touch Ten, or Jasmin. In her eyes they are scum. The rush of water as Maridadi lathers from the liquid dispenser, rubs her palms under the gush at the sink, is as rapid as Jasmin's heartbeat. The dryer couldn't be noisier. Jasmin stands at attention. Waiting for . . . what? She turns to look at Ten. The treacherous fool is gone.

Instead of walking out, Maridadi swerves into Jasmin. Presses her against the wall. Her honey eyes are searching for something. Shellacked nails tighten a burning grip on Jasmin's arms.

Jasmin's awareness is keen on the gravity, the texture, the shape of the other hand that is exploring her waist, her rapid breathing, her breast.

"What have we here?" says Maridadi. "It's a little mouse."

Jasmin's head clears. She stares at the starlet chain, all silver, dangling on the guard's collarbone. She tries to stay calm. "Everyone knows your truth," she says.

"And what truth is that?" says the guard.

"You speak soft but your stick is big."

Maridadi's soft laugh finishes with a wasp tail.

She smashes Jasmin against the wall. Jasmin feels the grind of guard's hips against her groin. The rock of Maridadi's hand still heavy on Jasmin's breast. The guard flicks her black tresses. Her honey eyes stay soft up close. Her smile when it breaks out is warm. "Jasmin. Isn't that right? I know about you too. Why, little mouse. You're trembling."

Jasmin finds her voice. "You planned . . ."

"I did. Ten knows to obey. Question is, do you?"

Inside the toilet, sounds of the machinery from the factory. Its incessant roar, hum, whine and titter. *Clatter-clatter-clatter. Zip-papa, zip-papa. Wroom-wroom.*

"And you think I have something for you?" asks Jasmin.

"Yes."

"Because?"

"What if I say—because I can? But it's more than that—put it this way: you scratch my back."

Jasmin speaks from Mandoza's lips, his bravery against the oppressor. But the words are her own. They are a recital. "Chemistry," she says. "You know when you lack it. The wrong kind is sticky, unpleasant." She spits her words. "Frankly, it's hell."

The guard's laughter, not a slap. "Little mouse is armed with talking points."

"Why do you hate?"

"But I don't."

Jasmin imagines the guard in another life. Confident, bohemian-clothed, easy. "What is it then? What you do?"

"Survival. It's important to keep it simple. Make clear who's at the top of the food chain."

"Killing your own people?"

Maridadi's hand drops to her taser. "Enough, or you'll be next." Her eyes are a storm. "We might be done here, but we're not finished yet."

Only as the guard boots away does Jasmin realize how rapid her breathing. Nothing can exorcise Maridadi's imprint on Jasmin's breast.

* * *

Jasmin feels eyes on her neck, continuously across her day: as she returns to the assembly line and Mama Apiyo waves her solidarity; as she nibbles at a boiled yam in the canteen and ruminates on the starch and sprinkle of palm oil; as she collects her coat from the main office and pockets her day's wage of a food voucher.

She walks with Mama Apiyo in the chill of the disappearing light. She slows her pace to accommodate the older woman's limp.

"Ten," asks Mama Apiyo. "What was that about?"

"Sucking up to Maridadi, is what."

Mama Apiyo's pale eyes study her. Her sag of cheeks has seen many tears dancing in the moonlight. "I know times are hard. But a spider's cobweb is both a bed and a trap."

"You have no need for worry. I know a spider when I see it, and Maridadi is not one. She lacks the cunning of it. What she is, I can tell you, is a hurricane. And that's a whole different matter. A hurricane doesn't contemplate who it strikes. It just strikes."

9

Today, as Jasmin collects her children, she has no wish to converse.

But Mama Gambo touches her gently on the arm. "Something is happening. In a few nights. I'll tell you to put the children to bed early and you'll do it, don't question it."

Jasmin nods. Doesn't ask why.

* * *

Back home, Mia and Omar are restless.

"Shiwo, Mamm. Shiwo," Mia.

"I want a big people story," Omar.

They demand stories—these children who've never seen a book. But they know literature, stories she has faithfully told them in oral narration.

"If you brush your teeth, change into your sleeping clothes, maybe, maybe then I'll tell you a story." She smiles at the alacrity of their heeding. She ponders about stories. Today they're primary colors dancing in her head.

The children are cross-legged on the mattress. Eye her with expectation.

"This is the story of the monkey's heart," begins Jasmin. "Shiro was a cheeky little monkey who lived with her baba. Their house was at the top of the old baobab tree. The tree had the brownest trunk and the greenest leaves. The tree was tall, tall, tall, and fat, fat, fat, and it stood on the bank of a giant, wide lake. Inside the lake was a big, bad crocodile, who was always lurking near the old baobab tree."

"Why was cwocolide lufting?"

"The word is 'lurking'—Omar, tell your sister what it means."

"It means to lie in hiding and wait. The crocodile was sly. He prowled about, hiding in the shadows. Lurking."

"Lufting. More cwocolide, Mamm."

"Well. Baba warned the cheeky little monkey. He said, 'Be careful of the long-toothed croc.' And did cheeky Shiro listen?"

"Shiwo. Listen."

"She did, for a while. One day, Baba went hunting for bananas, because Shiro loved to eat bananas."

"Nana. Yum," cried Mia.

"Yes. And Shiro especially loved the little, yellow bananas that grew at the edge of the forest. 'Stay home,' said Baba. 'Stay away from the big, bad croc.' And did cheeky Shiro listen?"

"Shiwo. Listen."

"No, she didn't."

"That's right, Omar. Shiro didn't listen. She was a curious little monkey and she waited for Baba to leave. And off Baba left, to find soft, sweet bananas from the great big forest. What happens next, Omar?"

"Shiro sits on the edge of the overhung branch of the old baobab tree. She peers at the lake, sees the long-toothed croc swimming and swimming around the tree."

"And then what, Omar?"

"The little monkey peers so hard, she falls from the tree!"

"That's right. But I think we'd best stop here, as it looks like our goatling is fast asleep. As you should be too, Omar."

"Mama, why are we?"

"We just are, my love."

"What makes guards?"

"They're just . . . guards."

"Why can't we be them?"

"Everyone has a purpose, my love. Maybe one day you might become a guard."

"I don't want to be a guard. Never."

"A supervisor or a teacher, perhaps?"

"I want to work in the mines and make loads and loads of mafinite! And then I'll be a king!" He looks at her with shiny eyes. "Are monkeys like us?"

"They . . . they think, they feel."

"Is their language ours?"

"It makes sense to them."

"Why are there no monkeys in Mafinga?"

"Mafinga doesn't have all the answers."

"Why doesn't it?"

"You, my goatling, have asked the last question for today." He allows her to tuck him in. "Shall I sing you a song?" He shakes his head. "Then I'll watch you until you fall asleep?" He nods.

Finally, the world of sleep gobbles him.

She touches his brow with her lips. She worries for him. What will become of him?

10

Sometimes stories flee her head as she lays quiet in the room. They bounce and swerve, careful of consequences. They leap and dive stillborn into turning pages of coverless books full of blanks. Her eyes are accustomed to darkness, but she needs the solace of text, of subtext that doesn't match the maps of a censoring system. She seeks to find meaning, but there never could be logic except in the contraband. She's entombed in dullness. Feels nothing as she stares at the blank screen of her mind, the bones of her anger fully broken.

At first, there was dissent, a few riots. After Baba Gambo, then what happened to the Elvis suit man, the people's anger fell to pieces. They understood that when a fish rots, the head stinks first. Mafinga was rotting, and King Magu reeked worse than century-old rot.

Now the people of Mafinga are condemned to a world of working, only leaving when a whistle says so. This is her certificate of presence: unquestioning, unthinking, just doing. Question it, and she's vapor. Unquestioning is her certificate of oneness with the system.

But Jasmin questions.

Sometimes she leaves this contemptible world with her mind to find places that are a vigil for someone lost. Half-revealed forms stir in the shadows. They say: *Don't fall, don't be afraid of the ghost.* But she's afraid of rats and snakes way more than she is of ghosts. So, instead, the forms say: *Don't bury the passion or let it ash. What's your passion? Please, don't fall.*

Is the ghost her lover Solo, lost in the king's mines? Or is it her late husband? There's a palimpsest under her pillow that holds imprints of Godi's words she's beginning to forget: *You're my one-way street, there's no wrong turn.* The room echoes with the timbre of words that will carry her to tomorrow, just like yesterday and the day before. She's aware of the balance, the rhythm and image of this moment's story that unfragments her memory of Godi and makes him whole inside her bristled heart.

But when she sleeps, she dreams of Solo who is never complete. She's an almostness without connection. An unknowable unknowing in a world that never is. It's full of light that never sleeps. Swept in darkness that's more than numbers. Jasmin dreams in language, the language of water, where Solo is a solvent. Her welcome is without maps, no barriers to her affection, it's an open tide.

Jasmin noticed the attraction in the factory, those days when Solo was a worker. There was clear polarity, charged both ends. The cohesion of their press, face to face, skin to skin, they swooned in the system's tension, gave in to simultaneous heating and evaporative coolness. They avoided mention of tragic folktales in the afterglow, of pale things of no consequence, of goblin questions without answers. That dawn, Jasmin—having sneaked into Solo's unit—fell asleep in their tangle of arms. But it was touch without nearness. She found her way back to her mattress, to her children. For a few months they were lovers, then the system hurled its malice. Solo, their brief togetherness cut short with a dispatch to the mines. They were forever mines, few people came out intact.

Their love now carries in a different place of invisible beds, each isolated by a bulge of water that burbles over Mafinga. A sonic hue is the sound it makes, rippling over tinted rocks and desirous hearts.

Unable to sleep, Jasmin pulls out the story machine. Surgical steel is the best, writes Shellon:

You carve out students from the text—these ones are continually redefined, unembedded in labels. A deeper cut and you get the physicians, self-experimental and resourceful. The poets come from a bleed. They work silently yet loudly along merits of paint, play and poeticity. But the teachers rise from a deboning. They toss about with itching, bloated faces and very sad moments. They're archaic, even perilous, restrained in methodology. You disrupt their ideas of fixed parameters, you destabilize their language—now a twig, or is it a thorn? Surgical steel is always the best.

11

Thursday.

Whoop. Whoop. The work siren goes. Doors open, doors close. The ritual. Mia and Omar to Mama Gambo's. The drudge to the factory—no one is in a hurry to get there. King Magu is up on the screen:

"Tomorrow is a rest day—this is the people's gift for the progress we have made in Mafinga. Ujamaa Factory is flourishing. Ujamaa Yaya is forming our children. Ujamaa Tech is engineering our future. The importance of our existence demands we do not incubate personal greed. Live the moral principles that embody the ideology of the people. Everyone has a right to equal work and a share of equal harvest. Tomorrow is a rest day."

"Equality?" snaps J. They are sitting on a bench in the cafeteria. "What about the guards, the supervisors? How is that equality?"

"It is transition," says Ten. "A framework of success."

"How is dominance success?" asks Bake.

"It's not dominance, just guidance," says Ten. "Soon we'll mature in Ujamaa and will need no direction to stoke the flames that will shape the future of Mafinga."

"What future?" asks Jasmin.

"Peace. One nation. These are things only possible when we don't choose for ourselves, but let the system choose for us. It's to our benefit."

"How?" J is getting agitated. The canteen and its boiled yams germinated in a factory is not a stress-free zone. The yams taste like the sunburnt skin of a hyena's bum.

Workers return to their assignments on the shop floor. Assembly line. Conveyor belt. Quality control. The production line is manufacturing nuts, rings, joints, hoses, pipes, adapters, fittings, connectors, tubes, cones, locks, hubs, compressors—small things for a big machine never assembled whole. Bitsies—nobody knows what they are forming. Even supervisor Hotel doesn't seem to know. Jasmin remembers the machine shaped like a human that crushed Baba Gambo.

Mafinga's turning was at first gradual. But the transformation coincided with the arrival of Atari. It was as if his very being was an assault on the state. Soon after his appearance, the essence of Mafinga started changing.

And it wasn't just the whole Ujamaa business. It was the sickness, the spewing out of plagues. First, the air went foggy. Then something black invaded the soft loam soil. Savanna grass calcified into rubble. Then it was the crops. Potatoes crumbled, black soil inside like a disease. Yam, bitterleaf, eggplant, spinach, pumpkin, black plum, Bambara bean, cowpea, rice, banana, maize, ground nut, sweet potato, sorghum, sugarcane—nothing was spared. They all shriveled and died. Even cash crops like coffee, tea, cotton all gnarled into a witch's finger.

The disease spread. The marula tree no more gave of its yellow fruit. The whistling thorn lost its music that came when the wind blew. The soft pulp of the quiver tree went hard as a barren womb. Grubs in the butterfly tree turned to pebbles and crashed to the ground. Even the baobab tree lost its towering. It hunched and faded to ash, to fog.

Alarm grew when roosters lost their feathers. They stopped crowing and fell from perches in fits, drowned in their own froth. Panic spiked when dogs first went bowlegged, then they too collapsed.

Cows began to lose horns, their hide molting but no new skin replaced it. They mooed hideously, their agony as flayed, ripe tendons, and then bones, became exposed. Suddenly, there were dead animals everywhere, and you couldn't eat them.

The whole place resembled the aftermath of an apocalypse.

Then the sun turned its deadly gaze on the men.

* * *

Jasmin collects the children.

"You heard?" asks Mama Gambo.

"Tomorrow is a rest day," says Jasmin.

"Good. I'll come to you with news."

Potatolux, then the children demand story time.

"Shiwo, Mamm. Shiwo."

"A big people story, Mama."

* * *

The children are asleep. Mia in little purrs. Omar in a noiseless coma that zombifies him. He falls into the world of sleep and it swallows him. Sometimes, in the depths of his gobbling world, he sleep-talks or -walks.

The world is going to sleep. It's the end rather than the start of day as it used to be. Toil has been and gone. The twisted world keeps turning as people lie still, after hours of bowing and scraping, of ritualized gestures that renew nothing but commitment to a system's propaganda. Theirs is a dream-filled sleep that will take them to the other side where no cloud has a silver lining. The rising sun is a looming bombard waiting to fire. It hovers in the sky as it makes up its mind how many more to exterminate.

* * *

In a pouch under her mattress is every note Godi wrote—they're jottings of things he wanted her to remember when he was gone. Like the taste of honey, a sticky molasses full of flowers and spice that increase the blood flow to her heart. Like the smell of coffee, a rich bitter burst of burnt chocolate that perks her spirit to possible futures. The feel of mud on her fingertips, a liquid denseness all soothing and dirty—it's a smear of vigorous pleasure. The rhythm of inked pen on perfumed paper: the nib twirls to a perfect symphony of soft drums, oboes and trombones. Each reading is a rush of leaves in the jaws of a playful wind but, abandoned ghosts, the notes are stacked away in the coffin of a pouch, waiting for her heartache to outgrow itself.

She thinks of the last time he took her in his arms. It was before sickness overtook him. Godi, her tall plushie. He was wearing in bed a wifebeater—as he jokingly called the tradie vest he adored. His eyes as he took her were a dawn-gray. Sometimes she remembers them as a blue-green gray in her head, how unusual they stood out against his dark skin. She wrapped her legs around his slender but athletic frame, dug her fingers into his short crop. The tenderness and urgency of his lips. Over and over she sees his weathered face, his smile that reaches and reaches, sometimes passing invisible notes about a time before the letting go. Today the memory of him is the aroma of durian fruit in the heart of starvation.

But sometimes, many times, he is stretched out to a barely remembered abstraction spoken in dream language. Reflections catch her in dreamscape and return her to herself. They remind her of specificity. Today she dreams of a scatter of Cabbage Patch dolls, each with threaded hair seamless sewn to skull, rounded cheeks and baby eyes. Their smocking dresses are ribboned and full of checkers, but others have sunshine frocks all peachy and tropical, rosy, lilac and minty flutters. The babies have mustard rompers or pajama tracksuits swollen with gummies, lollipops and sours.

She snaps to, fully awake, to the horror that's Mafinga and its fragments, abstractions and premonitions. She traces the outline of her life as it stirs to wakefulness at dusk.

12

Friday.

No *Whoop. Whoop.* The work siren doesn't go. No door opens or closes. No ritual. The children are still asleep. But Jasmin is awake. She feels her cramps. Her period is coming in a day or two. When it happens, the system will take care of it.

The toilet feels your temperature, examines your urine, spits sanitary pads from lips on the wall. It hasn't yet detected that Jasmin is not taking the supplements, but it's a matter of time. A chemical bin incinerates the waste. The units at Ujamaa Village are efficient this way. The system gives everything. The system takes everything. Even your freedom. A fine-tuning toilet that self-disinfects.

Like the toilet, the house adjusts itself. It dusts. It mops. It heats. It cools. You don't touch anything unless you must. If the system does everything, what use are you without it? What use are you in it?

So, rest day is a conundrum to many people in Mafinga. They don't know what to do with themselves. But recreation is no challenge to Jasmin. There's much to do with time when you have it. She has Mia and Omar. She hates to admit it, as it is system-run, but there's Ujamaa Facility. There's the story machine. She can take refuge in its precise words, those that tell her of Maupasso to whom memory is more perfect than the universe. Or Flaubeatrice who reads to live. Or Georgina Eliot who can look at a subject from various points of view. Or Wauf who understands that no gate, lock or bolt can set upon the freedom of her mind. Or Weller who can step outside the person she's been and remember the person she's meant to be, the person she wants to be, the person she is.

What person does Jasmin want to be?

Not this one, locked in a container.

She slips out of the unit while the children are asleep. It's dark outside. With such intermittent sleep, no wonder she feels exhausted. Every nerve in her body has a jump. She makes her way to Ujamaa Facility, uses her token. The scanner flashes green, lights come on.

Like all toilets in the system, this one has a ghost flush— self-cleansing, she doesn't have to touch it. But this is where the resemblance ends. Unlike the bidet in the unit, this toilet has a roll. The tissue is as soft as a lover's whisper. She plunges into the icy pool of a communal bathhouse that's nothing baroque. No spa or hot springs. No luxury of a mirror. No bolts or latches, not even a window. It's a shack, really. A shack with an ice plummet and a sizzler shower. But the lick of the water's frost in the plunge pool soothes the ache from her muscles. She tucks chilled fingers in her armpits.

In the shower, she tilts her face to the steaming hot rain, rubs the modest white blossom of hibiscus gel into her hair. The folded towel is soft and absorbent, nothing fluffy like a politician. It does the job and you drop it in a bin. The dryer's hum as it puts chaos to her hair. A choice of lotions: the lingering sweet floral of black tea; fresh woody musk of an orange blossom; licoricey scent of vanilla bean . . . She takes the green fragrance that reminds her of the bark of a baobab tree. So relaxed, she's ready to close her eyes and sleep.

There are a few people out now, but Jasmin doesn't want to make small talk. She makes for the shop, one of the units at the village. She arrives as the shop window swings up.

Ulafi pokes out her head. She has sleep in her eyes, crystals on her unwashed face. "What you want?"

"I was hoping to get a can of millet porridge, two eggs and a packet of boiled sweets."

"You can't afford it. Three months of food vouchers—you got those?"

"How about mafinite?"

Ulafi licks her lips. "I could keep it and report you."

"But we know you won't."

13

Omar sits up on the mattress. He eyes Jasmin with suspicion as she walks into the unit, her arms laden.

"Where did you go?" he demands.

"To have a shower. You want one?"

"No."

"Your sister is still sleeping?"

"Yes."

"You want to dress?"

"No."

"At least brush your teeth."

"Then you'll tell me a big people story?"

"First, we'll have breakfast."

She rips the cover from the can of millet porridge and puts it in the microwave that hums for a minute. She stirs the porridge to keep it nonsticky and is putting the can back for more heating when there's a knock. It's Mama Gambo.

"I choose to arrive where the milk is sweet," she says.

"I could do with some milk," says Jasmin.

"Tssk. If you don't have patience, you can't make beer."

"Your metaphors completely confuse me, Mama Gambo. How does sweet milk become beer? My children won't drink it. I wouldn't let them."

"Let me." Mama Gambo tastes the gruel. "What you need is creamy coconut."

"And give away my kidney?"

"Ulafi would enjoy that. Only the gods know how much that costs on the black market."

Jasmin cracks the eggs. She stirs egg yolk into the nutty taste of mash. She serves equal portions into four bowls. The unit is not equipped for visitors. It's not equipped for rest day. It is designed for sleep.

They sit in a circle on the floor.

Omar can't wait, he's gobbling his porridge.

"Chew before you swallow," says Jasmin. "Can you see how Mama Gambo eats slower?"

"She's old," he says.

Mama Gambo laughs. She takes another spoonful. "Mmmhh, let me die now. I've needed this for a long time."

"We'll have to wake the little one before her porridge goes cold."

Mia wakes on a whimper. She's clingy, grumpy. "Wee, Mamm."

"You go to the toilet by yourself, can't you?" Mia begins to cry. "If you stop being childish, I'll hold your hand."

Jasmin returns with Mia to see Mama Gambo looking at the door. The older woman casts her gaze on the children. "Let me take these ones," she says.

"Not today."

"Especially today. Someone is here for you."

Jasmin looks at who's entering. She gasps.

"Solo!"

Omar leaps with the swiftness of a gazelle, reaches the visitor first. He locks his arms around her knees. "Auntie!"

Mia is crying, her arms reaching. "Sowo!"

Jasmin has many questions—where to begin? Solo looks worse than a tramp, mine dust all over her face, flannel shirt, pale khaki overalls. She's carrying Mia, rubbing soot all over the child who doesn't mind.

"I thought . . . I'd never see you," says Jasmin, as controlled as she can.

"But why, Jazzie?" laughs Solo.

"The mines eat up people."

Mama Gambo's cough is discreet. She lifts Mia from Solo's arms. "Let *me* take the children."

"No! Mamm! Sowo!" Mia wriggles to be free.

"I'll tell you a story," coaxes Mama Gambo.

Mia brightens. "Shiwo?"

"Yes. Shiro."

Jasmin looks at Mama Gambo in disbelief. The older woman clicks her tongue. "And you thought you're only one who knows about the monkey's heart."

"Big bad cwok," says Mia.

"Yes," agrees Mama Gambo. "The crocodile was lurking in the waters, waiting to pounce. Like this!" Mia squeals, laughs, then sings: "Cwocolide lufting, lufting!"

"Let's go," says Mama Gambo. "You too, Omar. Come with me."

He cocks his head. "And you'll tell me a big people story?"

"I'll tell you any story you want," says Mama Gambo.

"Here," says Jasmin. "Take Mia's porridge. And her toothbrush."

"I bwash my teeff, bwash my teeff," sings Mia.

"You have my heart's gratitude, Mama Gambo," says Jasmin.

"Today, only today. I am the mountain you lean on."

"Take these." Jasmin hands her the packet of boiled sweets. "They are for the children. *Only* the children."

"Of course," says dogged Mama Gambo.

* * *

Now they are alone.

"Solo."

"Jazzie."

"It's really you." Jasmin touches Solo's unwashed braids. Runs fingers along the sooted face.

Solo traps Jasmin's hands. "I hear you stopped taking the supplements."

Jasmin pulls back. "Even you? What do you know?"

"Just enough."

"Why didn't you tell me?"

"Sometimes ignorance is respite?"

"Now you're a god!"

Solo's palm sings on Jasmin's face. "We've lost enough time for silliness."

Jasmin slaps her back. Their breathing is rapid. They fall into each other, fighting jackals as clothes fly.

Later, much later, Solo breaks the silence. "We have an insider in the palace."

"Who?"

"We don't know who it is yet, but the intel to the resistance is valuable."

"What resistance?"

"In the mines. There's a faction. We have means."

"To do what?"

"There's something about Atari. There's more than you think."

"And you know this now? He's always been up to something."

"We believe he has something to do with Mafinga's climate plague. What we want to know is how, and why."

"You must be careful!"

Jasmin thinks to her own doubts, her questions. The factory, all those seemingly purposeless nuts and bolts the workers are building and rebuilding.

"There's something else," says Solo. "Matatizo Triba, when her husband died. One night before Mafinga changed, she saw something odd."

"What was it?"

"It's rumors. You don't ask that one questions—she bit the cheek off the last person who tried."

"Well then. Leave it as rumors."

"They say she was putting flowers at the holy place, pouring millet brew for the gods, when giant lights shot from the sky, headed toward the red rock. She scattered in panic as a monstrous egg landed with flares, then the egg vanished and Atari pulled out of the rock."

"No wonder she's angry if people are saying all that about her. Anger and madness are kindred. Matatizo's mind is messed up for that nonsense. And with triplets in her tow, who can blame her?"

"Think, Jazzie."

"I'm thinking. Let's just go with the monstrous egg. If it collapsed from the sky in an inferno, why wasn't the holy ground blackened? It's not devastated."

Solo shakes her head. "I think Atari is an alien."

"Sure, he doesn't resemble a man—"

"How else do you explain the monstrosity?"

"Because he's an apparition with his golem head, it doesn't make him extraterrestrial."

"What more evidence do you need?"

"Enough to know you have a lot of time on your hands in the mines. We need a savior, not gossip. I think you've forgotten how it is in the factory."

"Jazzie. Do you really think?"

Jasmin looks at her long. "No. I'm sorry. Who can ever forget the factory?" She takes Solo's hands. "I just don't think Atari is from some galaxy."

"More like a black hole."

Jasmin thinks of the flying spacers the guards use. That's a lot of tech going into Ujamaa. And she's welcome to the idea that Atari burped out from the stars. Farted out, more like.

"Here." Solo presses a stone into Jasmin's hands. It's yet unpolished.

"Solo! How you risk things. It's a death sentence to smuggle yourself, let alone one of these out of the mines."

"Not much mafinite any more in the mines. It's depleting—loads to the castle every fortnight."

Just then, a siren, radiance as the village comes alive in a flicker of green, yellow, bronze. A cocktail of incandescent light.

"Guards!" cries Jasmin. "Run, quick!"

Solo falls out of the mattress, grabs her overalls and boots, is barely out of the door when a shot bigger than thunder blasts from the horizon.

THE ROYAL
HOUSEHOLD

1

It's not a plane or a chopper. It's an egg in the sky. It has no wings or feathers—just high tech that flickers green, yellow and bronze in a cocktail of light. The pilot is playing with a joystick, maneuvering the egg as if she's engineering the console of a gaming computer. Seemingly no effort to run it.

Granite enters Jasmin's stomach as the vessel glides to height like a smooth elevator, before it bullets forward. The dashboard is full of buttons, a few of them blinking. A seatbelt sign is on, red arrows flickering. But no one cares. Mia is off her seat, unbuckled as she may. She's resting her head on Jasmin's lap. Jasmin strokes the child. Omar is to her left, leaning on her shoulder. And to her right is Maridadi, handcuffed to Jasmin.

The options of execution are at the fore of Jasmin's mind. They will spare her children. They must spare her children. She thinks of ways to die. Arms and limbs crushed in the pulp machine. Perhaps there's a newer device that breaks a person bone by bone. Or saws you upside down. Flays you. Boils you. Impales you. She's thinking these things as she sits in the comfort of alien tech. A silent spacer that exudes a tail of heat as it coasts the horizon.

* * *

She should have known Maridadi would be the one, rocked up with Ulafi. When the door of her unit collapsed, it wasn't a bleeding Solo who fell back in. At first, Jasmin felt relief. Then she panicked, thinking that the shots had already disarmed Solo who was a beacon in that conspicuous mine garb with its flamboyant flannel shirt. She imagined Solo reaching from the ground for an angel of saving who would never come.

Maridadi spoke first. "I said I know about you, little mouse."

"What you know is dung."

"I also said we're not finished. I hear you're packing mafinite. Where's the rest of it?"

"I don't know what you're talking about."

"There's this." Ulafi held out the evidence.

"You, stupid dog," said Jasmin. "Barefaced hyena."

Maridadi looked about the unit. "I also hear you have visitors from the mines. They couldn't be far—where are they?"

Jasmin refused to answer. No blows to her jaw could scatter any answers from her lips. Bloodied, she watched as Maridadi and her dog turned the unit inside out.

"Look what we have here." Maridadi yanked the false bottom off the microwave. A smile played on her lips as she fingered the story machine. "I knew you weren't one to obey," she said in her assassin's voice that was a coo. "We hear a lot of these are floating in Mafinga. We'll find who's peddling them, every last of them."

"Then what?"

"Destroy them. Punish every reader—like what will happen to you in a minute. People have died for less."

Maridadi confiscated Godi's notes. The palimpsest under Jasmin's pillow with imprints of her husband's words. *Remember the taste of honey*, his breath against her skin. *Swollen with molasses and the nectar of sweet pea—a lily of the valley with soul notes of musk drizzled with apple*, nibbling her lip. As Maridadi pocketed the notes, Jasmin felt the violation and recoiled from it as if it were physical on her person.

The guard also took the mafinite—what time was there for Jasmin to hem the contraband into her tunic?

"The time for playing is gone. You'll tell me—where are the children?" Silence. "Your trouble is only beginning. It will serve you to cooperate. Who has the children?" Silence.

The blow took out Jasmin's jaw. But it was still there, searing her face. Somewhere inside her pain—as her ears rang—seeped a sound of commotion. It came from outside. Jasmin lifted her head from the floor splattered with her blood, cried out as Ulafi dragged herself into the unit, hauling with her Mia and Omar, both making quite a din.

"Mamm!" Hands reaching.

"Mama!"

The children struggled to get to Jasmin, but Ulafi held them back.

"They're just children," pleaded Jasmin.

A new guard shoved Mama Gambo into the unit. The older woman stared at the ground, her hands bound to the front.

"You know what this means," said Maridadi.

"Please, no," said Jasmin.

"The bitch's right," said Maridadi. "Release the old woman. Killing her will incite a riot. We only need one today." She glanced at the children. "One and a bit."

"I beg you."

"But it doesn't work that way, little mouse. Too late to start scratching backs now."

As the starlit night stretched into the horizon, Jasmin was a prisoner in a silent egg in the sky. Her fear of what would become of her, of the children, superseded her own fear of height. She looked down and saw the people of Ujamaa Village in a gather. They were gazing up at the egg blinking with incandescent lights as it climbed higher into the skyline with its cargo. The crowd stood hapless, perhaps with antagonism against the odor of a system whose malice was evident: how was snatching a mother and her two young children to some hell or other for the good of the people?

Jasmin wondered if, on the face of it, despite this crowd's

helplessness, some carried questions about what died, what lived, and the power of a crowd. If one were to go by the story machine, was it not a mob that walked the freedom march during the civil rights in a precursor to Martin Luther King Jr.'s "I Have a Dream"? Did not a mob rope and fell the Berlin Wall in a pivotal event of world history that witnessed the swoon of an iron curtain? It was a mob of children that took the lead in a gun control debate, participating in mass national school walkouts, one day forming a single protest swollen with over a million heartbeats and it caused the world to pause and listen.

She wondered if, one day, a turning point would swing without warning in Mafinga as it did in the author Mandoza's country. And when that happened, if the same mob that stood with limp hands and gazed with bleak eyes at dusk, and the egg soaring up the sky toward its scatter of stars, would finally tremble, come to life and find its roar.

* * *

Mia and Omar know something is wrong. What they don't understand is the severity of it.

"Mamm?"

"Yes, goatling."

"Member Shiwo?"

"Yes, my love. I remember Shiro. The cheeky little monkey who lived with her baba, their house at the top of the old baobab tree."

"Mama," says Omar. "The monkey already fell from tree."

"Yes, my love. And the big bad croc lunged from the murky waters and snatched the clever little monkey in his jaws." She looks at the children. "But the monkey didn't cry, because she was very clever." She runs her fingers along Mia's pigtails. "You two are very, very clever."

"I'm not going to cry, Mama."

"No kwai, Mamm."

Jasmin is carrying a deep hate and it is thought-focused. She thinks of the death throes of a star as a black hole ate it up. She thinks of a supermassive light that once upon a time shimmered in the sky. A burst of energy and a beast thrown as matter from a void. She thinks of Atari stepping out of a stone.

* * *

The stone leaves Jasmin's stomach as the egg slows, pushes down in a sudden drop until it is aground at the heels of a hill.

A bird that lands on an anthill is still on the ground, says Mama Gambo inside Jasmin's head.

Maridadi uncuffs Jasmin. She lifts her by the collar, throws her out of the shuttle and its luminous lights.

"Yes," spits Jasmin. "Molest me in front of my children!"

The weight of Maridadi's fist cracks into Jasmin's face. Another fist breaks her lip and the world stops as Jasmin falls. A dam bursts from her nose, and it's all crimson on the ground. She rolls her body, crawls away, reaching with her hand for . . . what? The kick collapses her guts and she stops breathing. She curls in her agony. The world spins. Through the haze, her hearing slowly finds clarity. The sound of her children's cries comes at her in a beast's jaws and it swallows her whole.

Somewhere outside herself, she hears Maridadi say, "Now we're truly done."

2

Trees like sticks, deadwood, arms asunder. They are white ghosts that peter out before the hill and a compound at its crown. King Magu's castle is bigger than the entire Ujamaa Village and its surrounding area, all the way to Central District.

Jasmin surveys what she can of the compound. Maridadi shoves her forward with a rough hand. She looks for the children, and they're behind. A guard is holding each by hand. Mia is skipping as if all is well. She's humming a nondescript tune forming in her head. Omar is silent. Perhaps he understands.

Thousands of stairs lead up the hill pulsing with fog. The steps melt into a walkway bordered with manicured lawns splashed in light. The land is patterned with wispy trees and their ghosts of leaves. At the top of the hill is a garden that sweeps all the way to a side building that serves as a courthouse—rumors of it and what goes on inside are rife. Stories of people who go through its entryway that's peaked with spikes and never walk out. The garden has bloodred flowers.

Unlike a typical castle, King Magu's world is a scatter of buildings, reminiscent of a chief's village. Each building is part of a circular fringe, the belly of which hosts a series of gardens. The rest of Mafinga is dying, but life thrives in this godforsaken castle. It's like a case of parasitic twins where the autositic twin feeds on the fetus of its sibling, draws oxygen from the sole pumping heart.

Along the compound are Ujamaa monuments of togetherness. Here are sculpted hands of a village holding aloft a toddler. Here, five women stir a pot, their palms touching on the spine of a giant spoon. Here is a throng of chiseled men reaching for a scythe. Here is a cast of vultures pecking into the lone carcass of a wildebeest on the ground.

Jasmin enters the courthouse and its long windows, golden drapes in hourglass shapes, bound at the waist by melancholy ribbons. She expects to see a crowd, titan as the one summoned to witness Baba Gambo's execution.

The room is empty, splashed with lights from a trail of monster eyes hanging off the ceiling. A single guard stands beside the queen on a dais. Finally, this is her. For the first time Jasmin is face to face with the second wife of King Chaka. The queen who is King Magu's stepmother.

Queen Sheeba is wearing a flowing gown blooming with proteas— they are rubicund and white. Her face is stern. A cascading-heart tiara brings out the small face, high cheekbones. Blood lips. Her hips are wide on the red velvet throne, hips that have never seen birth. Long black hair sweeps down her womanly shoulders and falls to the throne's lion paws.

It is with ceremony that the guard lifts off the tiara, replaces it with a black cloth on the queen's head. This is a silent hearing, realizes Jasmin. They mean to sentence her away from witnesses, to destroy her before anyone thinks to ask. For the good of the people.

She looks up at the gallery and sees the still form for the first time, up a floor, straight ahead, looking down on the proceedings. It's Atari.

Ara k'davra. A golem (/ˈɡoʊləm/ GOH-ləm) stands with inanimate eyes that spark to life when the air whispers a mythical tale of cruelty that involves speculation about the death of a soul. The brute is a machine of war. It grows weary when the maws of humaneness consume it, regurgitate it to years of wither until the promise of terror unkeys the golem's power of life. Is there such a thing as amorphous extroversion? No mask can thwart sacrificial calculus. When a golem resuscitates, it's engorged with a deep fondness for demons, ghosts and dybbuks. Scours streets to tear up children.

It was the novelist Flaubeatrice who wrote this in a story about a parrot, or was it about the memoirs of a madman?

"I've been watching you," says Queen Sheeba in a faraway voice.

Jasmin snatches her eyes from the golem at the gallery. "Mine is pain and suffering," she says in a deliberate way. Her face hurts with talking. "Yours is privilege."

"You would be defiant to the one who will pronounce your judgment?"

"I've done little to save Mafinga from your kind." Jasmin's words are a mumble from her broken lips. "Can I not speak now, be defiant, even when it's too late?"

"Better little than too late."

Mia is bouncing across the marbled squares, skipping and twirling around the court. She stops her bounce and stands on one leg. She dangles precariously, balances herself with spread-out arms, the wings of an eagle. She puts her foot down, stares at the dais with big, wide eyes. She pouts and picks her nose as she contemplates, distracting Queen Sheeba who is studying the child's antics.

Mia points. "Who that, Mamm?"

"It's the queen, stupid," says Omar in his grown-up voice. He looks at the queen, puffs his chest and makes his announcement. "I want to grow up and marry you. I want to be king."

Queen Sheeba's stern face breaks into a smile. She beckons him with a finger. A glitter on her wrist as her arm moves, a multipearl bracelet held together with white gold and diamonds.

"Then we'd better get to know each other first. Don't you think?"

"Yes."

"Come to me, child."

He climbs up the dais. Mia twirls after him. "Someone hurt my Mamm."

The queen places Mia on her lap. "Sometimes people hurt themselves." Chestnut eyes sweep across to Jasmin and back. The queen leans closer to Mia. "I hear you adore stories."

"Big bad cwok lufting." Mia toys with the queen's bracelet. "Shiwo live with her baba. Shiwo fall from a twee!"

"I don't know this story," says the queen gently.

"Bad cwok."

"Do you want your mother to tell you the story?"

"Shiwo?"

The queen looks at Jasmin. "Tell us of that which fell from a tree."

Jasmin has a good mind to tell the queen exactly where to shove her tree. But it is a command, and there's no need to worsen her plight. And the children's faces are lit, much expectation and trust in them. She bites her lip.

"The . . . um. Big bad croc lunged from the . . . um . . . murky waters."

"He snatched the clever little monkey in his jaws, Mama."

Something shifts in Jasmin. She lifts her chin in defiance, stares down the queen. "That's right, Omar. But the monkey did not cry, because she was very clever. She looked at the croc and said she didn't have her heart, and the heart was the best part of a monkey for a croc to eat. 'And where's your heart, little monkey?' asked the croc. 'I left it in the topmost branch of the old baobab tree, up, up there, right next to the blinky stars,' said Shiro, the little monkey. 'And why is your heart near the blinky stars, little monkey?' The monkey said, 'At the topmost branch of the old baobab tree, the blinky stars can reach the heart. And when they reach the heart, the gods can spice it up with good, good things.' And silly croc believed the little monkey. He thought Shiro had left her monkey's heart on the topmost branch of the old baobab tree."

"Croc opened his jaws and let the little monkey leap across his back and his tail," says Omar.

"Yes, and Shiro scrambled all the way up to her tree and called out loud from the top: 'Open wide, dear croc, open your great, big mouth for the god-loved heart.' The big, bad croc opened his mouth and the clever monkey hurled down a big, ripe mango."

"BOOFF!" says Omar.

"BOOFF!" says Mia.

"Yes, booff! right there on the croc's tooth. Do you remember what the big bad croc roared?"

Omar laughs. "'OH! How hard is your heart, little monkey?'"

"OH!" says Mia.

"And the clever little monkey rolled on the branch, as she laughed." Jasmin looks up, defiant, at the queen.

"Bravo. Bravo," claps the queen.

"Bwavo!" claps Mia.

Omar's eyes are serious as he gazes up at the queen. "Will you tell me a big people story?"

"Do you want the story about a tired old elephant that went rogue and it dragged a hunter across the savanna with its trunk, put the hunter's head on a log and crushed it?"

"I want another one."

"How about the story about an insect with giant wings that spread in a balloon, and it closed on naughty people's heads, and they couldn't breathe until they died?"

"Maybe another one."

"Then I have just the story."

Omar arranges himself on her feet.

"Once upon a time there was an Earth queen named Lira, and she was gifted by the gods. She breathed fire to warm her people on cool nights and set their pots alight so they cooked and feasted.

On hot days she breathed frost that made water so her people could drink the iced liquid that tasted of root wine and they danced. One day the queen took a walk in the savanna grasslands with her two-headed beast named Bichwa. The beast that was her pet snarled and gnarled at a bush. It gnashed its teeth and pulled out a hunter and the antelope he had caught from the shrubbery. But Queen Lira said, 'No, Bichwa!' before the beast could eat the poor man. His name was Twiga. He had the eyes of a giraffe and all its lashes. The athletic body you might find on a zebra, and all its rippling muscle."

"Did she marry the hunter?" asks Omar.

"Mawee," says Mia.

"In fact, yes. Queen Lira married Twiga and they lived happily for seven years, eleven months and thirty days. The queen had twin daughters named Dudu and Rain, and later a son named Luki."

"And then what?"

"In the eighth year of their marriage, the queen was once again with child and it was a difficult pregnancy. She was sick all the time and resented her husband. One day she invited Twiga to accompany her to the top of the mountain. He was pleased to be in her favor and was trotting with joy when she pushed him into the mouth of a volcano. She belly-danced and clapped her hands as he fell into the hissing lava and burst into flames. His dying howl shook the mountain a thousand times. Do you know how many a thousand is?"

"A lot," says Omar solemnly.

"That's right. The queen returned home alone. When the daughter Rain asked about her father, Queen Lira breathed her frost, and ice filled Rain's lungs. The daughter shivered, her limbs went stiff as wood, before her body snapped into ice-cold twigs and she died."

"And then?"

"The other daughter Dudu asked about her father. Queen Lira yawned out spiders from her mouth. They were big as fists and crawled all over Dudu. They spun webs with their fat legs full of hair until her whole body except her face was covered in a cocoon. The spiders sat their big round bodies on her eyes and nose, and hatched hundreds of eggs that were creamy and round and cloaked in wet silk sacs. Dudu couldn't breathe and she died, but not before the spiders pierced venom into her cheeks to rot her body so they could feed."

"Did Luki run away?"

"Luki wun," says Mia.

"Luki saw what happened to his siblings and started running. But the queen said, 'Bichwa get!' What do you think happened?"

"Bichwa ate up Luki's brain," says Omar.

Mia's eyes are wide.

"Yes," says Queen Sheeba. "As the boy started running, the beast put him to the ground in one lope, pinned him with its paw as he screeched. It sniffed the back of his head for a forever minute, then tore out his neck."

Mia's eyes are wider.

The queen looks at Omar. "Do you love this story?"

"I love this story."

"I yove, me."

The queen is still speaking to Omar, but her eyes are on Jasmin. "If Queen Lira could do such terrible things to the people she loved very much, how much worse would she do to a person who betrayed her trust?"

Up on the galley, Atari is gone.

The queen claps her hands. "Abebe," she says in her faraway voice.

For a moment Jasmin expects to see one of Mama Apiyo's sons rise from the dead. Abebe and Baako—they perished with the sickness. But the new bearer of this name is a tall, wiry woman, thin as a whisper. She appears as if from a wish and is dressed head to heel in mourning.

"Take the children to the nursery," says the queen.

3

The Queen's hands are clasped on her lap. She studies Jasmin and her bruised face, worse for wear across the evening, tingling from Maridadi's assault.

"I've decided what I'm going to do with you."

Jasmin looks at the queen. "How will you explain it to my children?"

"I hope you're handy with a mop and pail."

"What?"

"My last maid found herself cooked in a vat. Don't look so astonished. I never planned to kill you. I don't know what you think I am."

Jasmin draws closer to the queen. She stops short of climbing the dais. "You didn't get to hear the rest of the clever little monkey's story."

"Oh, I know it. The crocodile realized he'd been tricked, but he decided that he rather enjoyed the big, juicy mango. Baba returned from the forest with bananas for the little monkey. As she ate the sweet goodness of the yellowest bananas, the clever monkey told Baba all about the croc and the god-loved heart that was only a ripe mango." The queen smiles. "How's that for a finish?"

"It's . . ." Jasmin shrugs. "Polished. But you're still taking my children."

"They'll be fine. How much mothering do they need? There's this saying, what's that—ah: an orphaned calf licks his own back."

"My children are not orphaned."

"They will be if you're stupid. Now," the queen looks at her guard, "someone get the cuffs off the poor woman." She rises to her feet. "I gather you can walk by yourself?"

The queen's evening gown blooming with proteas sweeps to the ground. Her black hair is a sea that runs along her womanly shoulders, bobs and weaves to the generosity of her hips and sweeps to the back of her knees.

The queen is standing so close, Jasmin can smell her. She's wearing the aromatic scent of a flower partnered with musk. Woody notes, citrusy hue.

"Let me give you a tour of the land so it's clear you understand your limits," says the queen.

"Limits? For a woman accustomed to luxury, do you understand the meaning of the word?"

"Oh, my dove. How wounded. The answer is yes."

Queen Sheeba leads them out of the courthouse through a side door, out to the light-splashed lawns and gardens. Night will soon fade. She points at a pillared monolith with hoofed and winged multibeasts and gods etched on its walls. "That's the main castle."

"Where you and King Magu eat and sleep."

"I'm his stepmother. Remember that."

"There's no need to take offense at innocuous words. I could never forget such an important detail as your relationship with the king."

They circle the castle and reach a semidetached house. It stands separate from the main castle but is close enough to be an extension of it. "That's the cook's house and kitchen."

"Is this where you'll put me? Close enough to stay out of trouble?"

"You can wish."

They walk down a tarmac road shouldered by more lawns and wispy trees. The queen points out a circular marble building capped with a silver dome. "That there is Tech."

"Tech?"

"And that—" equally marbled and silver-domed, but this time twin circles are held together by a rectangular block between, "is Atari's lab. You'll do well to stay away from it."

"I'll take that advice." Jasmin faces the queen. "So—all this. You lack for nothing while people are cargo in tiny containers at Ujamaa Village. They leave those pitiful units to slave in a factory. Let me tell you about some good people. Hotel. She's a supervisor, but a generous one. She'll never be like your Maridadi—put that one in a leash! There's Mama Gambo. Every day she takes other people's children to Ujamaa Yaya. The sons and daughters that are not singing propaganda. Mama Gambo is a thoughtful woman, there's kindness in her look, in her words, in her touch. Now, *you* tell me how she can look at the children and not remember what you and your Atari did to her husband? All Baba Gambo wanted was the freedom to *have*, to *think*, to *be*. He never stole anyone's money; he worked hard for it. But you put him in a machine. Mama Apiyo's sons. Her husband. All dead. Mama Apiyo is the old woman at the factory. The one with a short leg. Watch and see how she slogs with the rest, doesn't lose her goodness. She keeps the factory running, not your stupid supervisors. And do you know about Violet? Her only crime was pebbles in her head. But they slayed her—a *mad* woman. That's what you and your system did. And you know what else you did? You took Godi. He was my husband, a solar engineer with much promise for Mafinga. Where's he now? Dead. *You* should know that," spits Jasmin. "Because I hear you visited Ujamaa Medico to make sure every single one of those boys or men was truly dead!"

The queen recoils, recovers. A mask on her face.

"Your tour of the land." There's bite in Jasmin's words. "This! If you care to know the conditions in Ujamaa—the village, the factory, the mothers, the children—how's this equality?"

"Asked by a true daughter of Mafinga. Did I tell you the story of an award-winning novelist who said in her acceptance speech: 'Inside my surreal joy is a malice. I hope some publishers are crying.

The ones who rejected this book.'" The queen's touch on Jasmin's arm is nearly a caress. "You see," she says. "I am also a storyteller. What I wonder is this: What's your narrative? Whose story are you going to shape?"

They are facing another garden with a childproof latch on its small wooden door. "Mia and Omar would love this," says the queen. She lifts the handle. "Enter." It's a children's garden with racing pathways and hideaways, dens and caves, water fountains and tree houses, molehills and valleys. "It's beautiful, right?"

"A beautiful coffin doesn't make one wish for death."

The queen's laughter is a tinkle. "All these gardens." She sweeps with her hand. "A very clever person looks after them. The play garden was King Chaka's gift to me. He had it built when we lost our first pregnancy."

Jasmin looks at her. "But I thought . . . ?"

"Everyone thought. Everyone thinks. I am not barren. What I am is worse. Do you understand how it feels? Have you lost a child?"

"You're making me lose them now."

"How is that the same?" Queen Sheeba swirls, her breathing fast. "How? Until it happens, until you're holding a dead child in your hands, how can you know? Each tiny coffin is a blade through your heart. At eight weeks she's the size of a liver. If she makes it to ten weeks, her body is in a jelly: little fingers, baby arms, legs limp in a wet sac. If she makes it to sixteen weeks, you can fit her in your palm. You look at her closed eyes and wonder about their color, at her glistening crown and wonder of the cornrows you might have braided on it. You wonder about the toddler she might have been— the galloping kind? The little girl she might have been."

Fat spider trees run along a tiny lake, fully shallow with artificial streams. On the water's surface are floating lilies. The lake is so clear, Jasmin can see rocks on its bed.

"When you lose a child," says the queen. "The cramps, the weakness, the fever of the ejection are not the worst of it. Your breasts are still tender, the nipples perhaps leaking. How can you forget? The grief of a child has no stages. It goes beyond the tawny fingers of denial, the crimson flame of fury, the navy ocean of melancholy. Past the gray smoke of deadness is guilt. That's what. Guilt. The lead weight of it. And shame. The plain knowledge that you can't be woman to your core if you can't fulfill the simplest thing that Mother Earth begs of you. To procreate."

The queen's eyes are shining. "But for that to happen one more time you must part your legs and expose your shame. The shame of a body infected with unforgiving. The shame leaking out of your womanhood. A lingering odor no matter how long or how often you douche. It's still leaking in a great trek to soil your dignity. You'd rather die than let your husband between your knees. He wants to please you, but what he's doing is another humiliation—a little worse than before, because this one, especially this one, you can't tell him. So, he raises his face with wounded eyes that tell you he thinks, he knows, that yours is a forever mourning."

"And he's right," says Jasmin. "It's that, and more."

"The terror each time you fall pregnant." The queen clutches her stomach as if in agony. She looks about to throw up. "Thinking this child will also die."

Jasmin feels overwhelmed. She glances at the play huts and picnic shacks, all made of wood. Sculptured goblins and fairies line the jaws of rock tunnels and mazes. Random sprinklers squeal with squirts of water, as they would to startle a child. Past a bunch of tree ferns, and then cane trees, a palm tree next to a sandpit with a hammock. Jasmin sits on it, swings on it for a moment. She closes her eyes to the sky.

"This garden," she says as if in a dream. "It has a strong sense of absence."

"The sounds of children will fill it. Mia and Omar—" begins the queen.

"The absence of *birds*," says Jasmin harshly.

They don't speak as they leave the garden. Toward the exit is an ancient tree, gnarled and coned like a witch's hat. The queen sits on a tree stump.

"Yes. I'm still mourning. But don't ask me why I'm wearing kimono sleeves shaped in butterfly wings, why I'm sweeping the palace with a wide, flowing looseness. Don't ask me about my closet, its evening gowns with fashion that's off-shoulder or fruity. You'll not find the colors of mud in my wardrobe. No hue of moss and seaweed, never mint, olive or lime. Nothing carob and umber, never caramel, cinnamon or gingerbread. No fossil and ash, never porpoise, dove or silver fish. My evening gowns are twirling with color. But it's a forever mourning that hurts no less."

They're standing outside a shoebox studio.

"Why are you telling me this?" asks Jasmin.

"I thought you might understand."

"You were mistaken."

They glare at each other.

"I'm keeping your children. And there's nothing you can do about it." The queen pulls something from the pockets of her flared gown. "But this you can keep."

Jasmin stares at it in disbelief. It's her story machine—the one Maridadi took.

4

The shoebox is Jasmin's new home, the kind a nun or a monk might inhabit. Ten square meters. A single bed, double pillows, linen all white. A wooden chair. A chest of drawers in the shape of a piano. An ensuite with a simple shower whose modest sprinkler offers nothing like rain. A toilet you flush by hand—it has a handle on the cistern. Even the towels are white as clouds. It's as if someone has forbidden color. But there are splashes of it in the striped quilt—reddish-brown and taupe. In the canvas painting—blood circles, indigo bruises. It reminds Jasmin of a scream.

A Heidi dress is laid out on the bed. A flowing thing that runs down her waist and reaches just above her knees. More of them in the closet. Khaki-colored things, no belts, just front buttons racing all the way down. They differ from each other in their sleeves. Cap sleeves, just off the shoulder. Three-quarter sleeves to just below the elbows. Half sleeves. No sleeves. They are all the right fit. Someone has taken effort to prepare for her coming. Either that, or Jasmin is the same size as the servant girl who wound up in a vat.

A filter of morning light spreads into the room. Jasmin smiles wryly at the conclusion of her first encounter with the queen. "Cementing terror with a personal approach?" she'd told Queen Sheeba. "You think you can call a dog and it will come while you're still holding a whip? You have a running balance. I want my children back before I start charging interest."

"The sun might set with fresh news," said the queen. "But you're in no position to make threats. Until then, good night. And don't try anything stupid."

"Like what?" asked Jasmin.

"Like lock yourself in. I always keep spare keys."

A lioness will protect herself from the flies, says Mama Gambo in Jasmin's head.

"I am not a fly," says Jasmin to the empty cottage.

Before dawn she gasps with pain as her pelvic walls break and her period flows.

5

She wakes at dusk, ropes twisting inside her body. The sanitary pad she found in the tiny bathroom is again soaked. The shower is pitiful, but it washes some of her pain, her indignation at the queen. She steps onto the mat, and is rubbing her hair with the white, white towel when there's a knock.

It's Abebe. The tall, wiry thing, thin as a wish. The one that took away her children. She whispers in with a tray.

Jasmin studies the woman, her funereal clothes—a black matron dress. Her hair like a hillock full of corn. "What are you to the queen?" she finally asks.

"The cook, the butler. To you, I'm the boss," says Abebe.

"I report to you?"

"Everywhere is out of bounds unless I tell you to go there."

"I want to see my children."

"Bedtime only. I'll take you then." She sets down the tray. "You might want to eat first."

Jasmin falls on the stewed fowl, fully skinned and peeling off the bone. Abebe has served it with cassava (twice cooked, the woman said with pride, steamed, then seared) and a slime of leaves with a bitter aftertaste.

"So hungry," says Abebe.

"Does a tooth see malice?" says Jasmin, her mouth full.

"When you're dressed," Abebe eyes the towel with disdain, "come to the kitchen."

* * *

Jasmin is handy with a mop. But there are white walls and white doors in the castle. Mirrors everywhere. The first bathroom on the upper floor is lit with a square plate overhead, protruding with four eyes that are bulbs. The room has a gilded tub and gold faucets. Hanging potted plants. The marble floor is patterned in squares. There's a plush rug to step on, candles to illuminate the toilet.

White and gold, the trimmings of the house. A polish of marble everywhere. Golden rails and curtains that wear a deep red velvet; they open and close at the press of a button.

She is dusting and mopping rooms with giant spider chandeliers in white and gold. Portraits of flowers, each regally framed like a monarch, line the walls. Here is the daisy princess, her white face and green veins, yolk inside her petal. Here is a water lily, her heart shape in jade against white.

The bedrooms are full of dust but lavish. Glass lamps to polish. Cream sheets to change. Golden quilts to spread. Baby vases filled with flowers to water. No sight or sound of the children, or the queen. Somewhere in a timeline along Jasmin's cleaning, Abebe summons her to the kitchen where she has laid out a bowl of spiced rice and fish soup.

"Tilapia," says the woman. "Eat quickly, and we'll go see the children. I don't know why he's let her keep them."

"The king?"

Abebe laughs. "King Magu is the least one to fear."

Jasmin considers the words. "I never imagined Atari had that much power," she says.

"Oh, he does," says Abebe. "If you knew the one thing he allows the queen to keep. It's his hold on her."

* * *

Jasmin follows Abebe up a winding staircase, mahogany and

shimmering with sheen. She wonders what hold Atari has on the queen. They climb all the way to the northeast tower of the marble-coated monolith.

The children's nursery at first feels like a basement tavern with faint music in the background. It's an odd melody, the hiss of a snake and a soft clash of cymbals. As her eyes acclimatize to the dimness, Jasmin sees the room clearer. Its pillars rimmed with gold, each boasting a bracelet of orange-flamed candles at half-mast. It's a large room of arched doorways. Along the walls are dimly lit paintings inside veils of cloud. In each is a version of the Garden of Eden. Eve leaning toward a behemoth serpent. Eve offering a glowing red apple to Adam. Eve and Adam running off naked from an ash-haired god who is a voluptuous woman full of breasts. There's no sign of the queen.

Jasmin catches sight of the children and her heart plumps. Abebe ceases to exist. Mia is crawling along the slippery floor with a gold and black train the size of a grown rabbit. Omar is bent over a puzzle piece box, turning and twisting, fitting colors to match.

"My goatlings." There's a frog in her throat. "Are you behaving?"

"Mama."

"Mamm. I bwashed my teeff."

The children tumble into Jasmin's arms. Mia is wearing a unicorn pajama set, tiny shorts and a T-shirt. Omar's has all-over flying dragons.

"Roar!" he cries. "I'm a dragon! Let me breathe you some fire!"

Now they're giggling, helpless, tickling each other on the polished wooden floor.

"Look, Mama." Omar gives her a tour of the nursery. The beds are tents in lollipop colors. Mia's little mattress inside her tent is light, puffy. "It's a soufflé cot," says Omar in his serious voice. The bed linen is full of yellow lions with giant manes walking on golden grasslands. Summer pillows swell with patterned rims of the sun on them. There's a towel with a giraffe hood. Next to a chiffonier is an alien-looking fist, gray skin like the bark of an ancient tree. Inside the fist, is a kaleidoscope of lights in a marble.

"What's this?" asks Jasmin.

"It keeps us safe," says Omar.

"Who gave it to you?"

"I tell. Me, Mamm!"

"No!" roars Omar.

Jasmin sits back. "What's this then?"

"It's a secret. We can't say about him."

"The king?" It could never be Atari. Or could it?

"Mama, we can't."

"Member Shiwo?"

"Yes, goatling, I remember Shiro."

"Stowee, Mamm."

"Where are Hope and Art? Imani, Lia and Sabre?"

"Do you miss them, Omar?"

He nods. Mia nods.

Jasmin kneels and clasps them in an embrace. "Why, my goat-lings, they are in Ujamaa Village, remember?"

"Member?" says Mia.

"Mama Gambo's there too. Isn't she the best?"

"Best," parrots Mia.

"Your friends are fine, Joko and the rest." She looks about the room, notices the large windows. "Goodness, you have a view!" She stands to explore it. She can see the face of Atari's lab, the rectangular bit. As she looks on, she's astonished that the lab is moving. Now she's facing a dome.

"It goes around, Mama."

"Really." But even as she speaks, it dawns on her. The children's nursery is slowly moving, a snail-paced merry-go-round. Now she can see the face of her shoebox studio. She realizes the room has a specially fitted floor. It revolves, a sundial along a circular platform. The queen offers more lavish than Jasmin could ever afford.

She turns to the children, breathless. "Are you ready for this story or not?"

"Stowee, Mamm."

"Good, a story then. Let me tell you about Shiro and the lion cub." She sits on the floor.

"Shiwo." Mia snuggles between Jasmin's feet.

Omar is toying with the puzzle piece box, turning and twisting, fitting colors, but he's listening.

"In the wide savanna, there lived a bunch of cousin monkeys that loved to climb and play in the leafy trees."

"Cousin?"

"It means they were related. Like you and Mia. Now Shiro the cheeky monkey was the most playful. Sometimes, the monkeys saw Simba, the lion cub, prowling in the grasslands. When the monkeys saw Simba, they would cry: 'Hide, hide, little monkeys!' And they would scamper and hide inside the leaves, until the lion cub went out of sight."

"And then what?"

"One day the monkeys cartwheeled and swung on their tails in the trees when the lion cub appeared. 'Hide, hide, little monkeys!' But Shiro was curious and swung from branch to branch and leapt to the grass on her hands and feet. 'What's going on, lion cub?' The lion cub said, 'I have a plan. And my plan is—I'm going to get you!'"

Jasmin jumps and grabs Mia, who squeals. She settles the children into their tent beds, is loath to leave them but she must. Soon it will be light.

* * *

Outside the castle, she's half blinded by the moonlight across pedicured lawns. She sees green smoke wafting out of a chimney on Atari's lab, the twin circles capped with silver domes, a rectangle room connecting them.

Suddenly, a strangeness overwhelms her. She's walking in slow motion, her senses distorted. Her limbs are dotted lines. Her breathing is too loud, gasps in her ears. She's aware of the domes as they glow at her approach. They are swaying, shifting with obscure meaning. She feels they want something. Jasmin recognizes the sound as the golem spreads in a melt her way. It's a factory song.

Before she knows it, the walls are slipping, bricks peeling from the house, curling into the now sea green smoke wafting in her direction. Sound explodes syllable by syllable, the factory song now a shout: *Clatter-clatter-clatter. Ticky-tock-tock. Zip-papa, zip-papa. Wroom-wroom.* The golem is inside her head. Run, Jasmin, run.

She finds her feet. Run, run. Jasmin is running. Run. Run.

6

Abebe works her like a slave. Feeds her like an empress. Now it's goat meat and pounded bananas, served with peanut gravy.

Jasmin retches, struggles to hold in the food, right there in the uppermost floor, at the smell of animal vomit, rotting fish, or is it ancient excrement? It is seeping from a room with a closed door. There are people talking inside. Her curiosity gets the better of her.

She knocks lightly, steps in with her mop and pail before anyone can say no.

She nearly falls at the sight of the king. It is the king, isn't it? He looks nothing like what she sees on national broadcast, the shameless man with his propaganda in monotone speeches. The man in this room is covered in purulent boils, leaking yellow. A cloaked figure is nursing him by the regal bedside, basin and bowl, wiping the king's face gently with a wet cloth. Passes a bucket into which the king coughs up phlegm.

Jasmin sees a discarded leg on the floor. And then another, green with gangrene, by the bed. The king is a torso. He's falling apart in decay. One ear is twisted, trapped to the head by a gnarl of skin. It dangles, a zombie's appendage. The gaping orifice where the ear should be has a weepy creamy substance oozing from it.

The cloaked figure turns, finally aware of a visitor, freezes at the sight of Jasmin.

"Not here, please. Leave us."

The voice, thinks Jasmin, something about the scratch.

She walks out in a daze. How could that . . . that . . . pus-filled *thing* be King Magu? And who's that person with the king? It isn't Abebe or the queen.

Throughout, as she scrubs, scours, polishes, vacuums, the import of her discovery grows. The king is dying?

Procrastination will not fill the grain store, says Mama Gambo in her head. *You must act.*

Jasmin is distracted, her mind a scatter of ashes. To act, she must. But how? She can't leave the castle to tell the resistance—what will happen to Mia and Omar? The queen would gladly keep them. And how does one reach the mines?

She's still preoccupied as she gives the children story time.

"'I'm going to get you,' roars the lion," says Omar. Today, he's carrying the story, not Jasmin.

"Yes. Yes," says Jasmin absently.

"But the monkey did not cry, because she was very clever," says Omar.

"Yes. She . . . um . . . she looked at Simba and said she didn't have her heart, and the heart was the best part of a monkey for a lion cub to . . . um . . . eat."

"But the lion cub roared with laughter," says a faraway voice. The queen is wearing a Grecian open back that hugs her wide-hipped shape. An aroma of flower and musk enters the room with her. She kicks off her sandals, sits on the floor. Mia climbs onto her lap without invitation. Omar is curled at the queen's feet. "The lion cub said, 'I've heard that story before, how you tricked the big bad croc and hurled down a mango instead of a monkey's heart.'"

"What happens now?" asks Omar.

"The lion cub says, 'I will ROARRR! And pounce!'"

The queen grabs Mia and Omar, and they squeal and tumble together on the floor.

Jasmin looks at Omar, how at ease he is with the queen. Mia

cradled in the hook of the queen's arm, the trust in her tiny hand clasping the queen's fingers. She notices for the first time that the nursery, the pillared monstrosity of it, holds up a ceiling embossed with calligraphy she can't read, and lionesses in all manner of form. Sleek cats chasing down wildebeest, now mating with big-maned lions, now sprawled in a nap as fat-pawed cubs, whiskers stained with blood, pull at their mothers' breasts.

Jasmin feels like death. "I'll just go."

She kisses each child on the forehead, avoids Queen Sheeba's eyes.

* * *

In her cottage, she wanders about the kitchenette she hadn't taken time to fully notice. There's a tiny fridge, a toaster, a boiling kettle near the sink that's all silver. Inside a cupboard are wine flutes and china and bowls. On a tiny table is a baby vase with yellow flowers, real flowers with their perfume scent, freshly watered. Beside them is a jade bowl of dry leaves and decorum. Jasmin feels the dry leaves inside.

She takes the story machine from where she put it at the top of a chest of drawers molded in the form of a piano. She studies the gadget. A simple device with its flat face and dials, yet so powerful it scared a monarch enough to ban it. She cradles it to her chest, rocks it as she would a child. She picks a reading in which Georgina Eliot compares grief to a vast universe.

Jasmin surfaces from her misery and remembers the story of fate—the author Mandoza wrote it. The tale is of a man from Turkey who studied as a journalist but fled from conscription to stow away in a boat destined for Europe. He unfolded from his sleep, crawled out of a barrel, and straight into Bioko, an island off Cameroon's coast. He tried his hand at catching catfish, then cutting trees in the African forest. He got bit by a shrew but lived to make it as foreman.

A photojournalist from France looking for a helper with knowledge of the rain forest took the foreman and saved him from cutting the canopy and devastating the homes of the red-eared monkey, the island's eleven primate species, counting the black and red colobus. The helper worked as an apprentice and then specialized as an expert, made dollars to buy passage to Australia. He crawled out of a water tank, empty because he bribed, and took himself to a refugee center in Woomera, 446 kilometers north of Adelaide, where they locked him up for six months then granted him asylum.

The journalist, then stowaway, then foreman, then helper, then again stowaway, then refugee became a driver in South Australia and chattered his story to a writer who climbed into his cab in a rush to an annual literary event. The author restrung, retuned the story, slaughtered fact, bled fiction, chucked in some poetry. The artist was shortlisted for an award with that book, and continued to be an apt listener to cab drivers.

Jasmin looks out the window, at the wash of the yellow sun rising on the horizon. She thinks about walls of mirrors, laughing children falling out of them. She sees water fountains and tree houses. Floating lilies on a tiny lake where children bounce in bare feet. She thinks of the garden with its ancient tree, gnarled and coned like a witch's hat, and its strong sense of lacking.

Jasmin feels lacking.

Suddenly, out in the sun (*in the sun!*), she sees a pensive figure, cloaked and tall, strolling in a walkway between gardens.

* * *

The next evening, she waits with her mop and pail, gagging at the terrible smells of a corpse seeping out of the king's chamber. She stays until the cloaked figure steps out of the room, shuts the door gently behind.

He's startled. "You? What are you doing here?"

This close, it's Jasmin's turn to be surprised. "Why, you're a man!"

"And you've seen a man before, I'm sure."

"Yes . . ."

"There's a 'but' coming."

"But I saw you walking in the sun."

"It's a perfectly normal thing for a person to do."

"Not in Mafinga, it isn't. Are you a sorcerer, like him?"

"Him?" Before she can answer it dawns on him. He laughs. "The alien is us." He looks at her from the eyeholes of his hood. "But I give it to you—your imagination is vivid. I'd best leave you to it."

"Wait!"

He turns.

"I feel . . . Do I know you?"

"There's always a sense of déjà vu. Don't let it fool you, lest it tie you to a rope, leave you dangling from the moon."

He walks swiftly away.

7

Much on Jasmin's mind as she enters the Tech building with her mop and pail. There's the matter of the dying king. And that of the cloaked man. What's his potential to Jasmin—is he a friend or foe?

Inside the marble building with its silver dome is a toilet, a kitchenette, almost like the one in her shoebox studio. Unlike Ujamaa Tech, here people have liberty and there's nothing factory about the glass-windowed office full of monitors.

A bunch of teens huddled around a big screen pays no notice of her as she goes about scouring the soiled toilet bowl spattered with mud colors. There are stains of urine on the floor. She thinks of Godi. He peed straight.

She finishes her cleaning—you could eat off the toilet in that state, she muses. She steps inside the office, says, "This won't take long."

"No dramas," says a teen with a crop of spiked hair tamed with wax.

Unlike their seeming laze around the monitor, clearly, they've been at work—at thought, more like. It's not a brainstorm, Godi once joked. It's a "thought shower." Someone has scribbled on the whiteboard:

Mutuality is birthed by cooperation.
Cooperation is a descendant of equality.
Equality emphasizes mutuality.

The teens, not nearly seventeen, Jasmin is sure, are arguing.

"Sounds better on-screen if we say: 'Increased cooperation enkindles equality as the fundamental instrument to eradicate tribalism's associated conflicts,'" says a boy wearing blue jeans at half bum, starry boxers out. He's pimpled—angry little shits pushing out of his face.

"No, Soho," says a punk-haired girl. "We need to emphasize safeguarding against domination. We can get awesome video effects to go with that."

"Here, check this out," says a girl with big, round spectacles. She calibrates an image of King Magu on the screen, paints in battle gear so he's holding a shield and wearing a leopard skirt. "Bad ass, hey? This look goes with any slogan."

"Come on, Punk. A stabbing spear is better than a stupid shield," says the one with specs.

Jasmin's head is swimming. Soho. Punk.

"A stabbing spear? Yeah, is that even a thing?"

"Dog, you never support anything!"

"Stop it, bitches," says Soho. "What King Magu needs . . ."

"Is not a bunch of idiots!" cries Jasmin. "Soho? Punk? Dog? You little shits. And you," she points at the boy with the spiked hair, all waxed. "Is your name Smog?"

"That's not cool."

"I'll tell you what's cool?" Jasmin moves in their direction, stumbles on her pail. Water sweeps across the floor. It spreads toward the cables.

The teens fall on the mess with dusters, wipes, tissues, kitchen towel, anything. Smog pulls off his T-shirt to unveil a six-pack, guns on his arms. "You want to kill us?"

"Completely!" Jasmin lunges for the nearest throat.

Cold, steel fingers hold her back. It's Abebe, strong.

Jasmin is spluttering, livid. "Mafinga is dying! And these, these wooden-heads!"

"They are specialists," explains Abebe calmly. "Soho does sound tech. Punk is chill with cameras. Junkie, *not* Smog, no one gets him, but he knows makeup. And Dog is behind the slogans."

"*Children* behind the propaganda?"

"You're interrupting something important at personal risk," says Abebe.

"And peril," says Soho.

"You came up with Ujamaa from a bunch of *teens*?"

"Losing it on us, bitch," says Dog. "We keep the system rolling."

"Yeah, the whole resettlement idea," says Punk. "So cool."

"Because?" snaps Jasmin.

"It's about a socioeconomic profundity," says Dog.

"Yeah. Ujamaa means utopia," says Punk. "Togetherness. Communitization."

"Communi-what!"

"Instilling fundamental values," says Abebe. "Ujamaa is something to occupy the people, keep them from bedevilment or revolt."

"Coercive persuasion?" says Jasmin.

"It's Freudian," says Soho.

"What it is, is called menticide. You're exploiting people, hindering their capacity to think so you can enslave them with factory work. The metals, the bolts—what are they for?"

"Machines to mine uranium. Mafinga has loads," says Soho.

"Who wants it!"

"China," says Dog. "Russia. North Korea. Atari."

"It's all in motion. Soon, we'll close Ujamaa Factory," says Soho.

"Yeah. We have enough equipment."

"And what will happen to the factory workers?" asks Jasmin.

"We'll migrate them to new uranium mines. Ujamaa Village is designed so it can move, no dramas."

"Move the village—to where?"

"To the edge of Mafinga, at Red Rock. That's where the uranium is."

Jasmin thinks of the giant red rock, rugged, ridged, grooved and full of caves. Villagers stepping out of stones like bush people, alien eyes empty. "You want to put people in a desert full of stones?"

"We want them to mine uranium."

"Do you know the dangers of radiation? Lung cancer! It eats you outside in. Radioactive decay! Also linked to lung cancer. And the contaminate from drinking bad water gives more cancer! Like of the bone. And we haven't got to physical trauma from mining injury, or hearing loss."

"Sacrifices must be made," says Abebe. She releases her grip on Jasmin. "Now get working."

* * *

Mia and Omar fall into her arms in the children's nursery. No sight of the queen. Jasmin pushes out her distraction, obliges Mia and Omar with story time.

"So where were we, my goatlings?"

* * *

She avoids Atari's lab on her way to the studio. Feels something at the back of her neck—swirls.

"You, again. Are you following me?"

"Why would I do that?" says the cloaked man.

"To answer my question! It's a sham. This whole Ujamaa thing. Children running a pantomime."

"That's not a question."

"Is it Atari? Behind it all?"

"Yes."

"The king is dying?"

"That's a question I cannot answer."

"Can't or won't?"

"If we start with what you know, maybe I can fill in the rest," he says.

"There's nothing wrong with the sun. Either that or there's something special about you."

"It's engineered, nothing more than brainwash."

"What does a sorcerer want with uranium?"

"I thought you were cleverer than this. Atari is no sorcerer but a mage of fools. Only a fool cannot see what he's up to."

"And he's up to—what?"

"Creating something for his people."

"Who are his people?"

"We're yet to find out."

It dawns on her. "It's you. The insider. You haven't told the resistance about the king, how he's dying."

"Everything has its time. And there's still Atari. You've seen what he's capable of . . . We can't jeopardize more of Mafinga's people."

"Soon there'll be no one to protect. They want to move the people from the factory to uranium mines. Move Ujamaa Village, endanger every woman and child with radiation. For the good of the people!"

His shocked silence.

"How could you not know? You're right here," she says. "Under their noses. We must tell people there's nothing wrong with the sun. Tell them the system's plan to endanger everyone. We must fight this." She looks at him. "Go to the mines, start with the resistance. Tell them!"

"They will notice my absence. My room is right next to the king's chambers. He needs me."

Her gaze is quizzical. "You sleep in the main castle."

He looks a bit awkward. "I calm his madness."

"With stories?"

"Stories, yes. But discussing the king is never pleasant."

"What would you rather talk about?"

"The resistance. It takes time to arrange communication. But I can plan for you to slip away. You'd be back before they noticed."

"How can I reach the mines?"

"I know a way. They send someone from the mines to deliver mafinite to Atari here at the castle every fortnight."

"When's the next delivery?"

"In over a week."

"We can't wait that long."

"No."

"The king in his condition hasn't much need of it, and mafinite is no longer a currency except in the black market. What does Atari do with it all?"

"I haven't answers to many things. You'll have to trust me."

"But the children!"

"They're safe. I promise."

"And the queen?"

"She's not what you think."

Gustave Flaubeatrice wrote about demons. The beast is banality, conforming to an ideal you cannot confirm. The beast is listening to a story you don't believe. The beast is the meager, and it's worse than an empty park tormented with fiends. The beast is not knowing a name.

"At least tell me what to call you."

He considers for a moment. Then: "Tolkien. Call me Tolkien."

8

The ivory-white door on the rectangular face gives. It's been waiting for her. Inside is darkness. Jasmin clutches her mop and pail, her excuse to be here.

But this is a perilous snooping. This is Atari's lair.

Her eyes take long to understand the darkness. She puts down her pail at the entrance, feels the lab's walls with her fingers. There's a murmur in the air, a smell of burning. Jasmin turns left, feeling the walls toward the circular part of the lab. The acrid smell stings her eyes, her nose.

Slowly she makes out a colossus vat in the middle of the lab. It's almost the height of a person, but half a room wide. And suddenly, there's laughter. Without warning, bursting out like a nursery rhyme in cartoon is the factory song. *Ticky-tock-tock*. *Wroom-wroom*. The sound is deafening. *Ticky-tock-tock*. *Zip-papa, zip-papa*.

The smell of burning after burning. Jasmin can't believe her eyes as a skeleton of bird nests rises from the smoke. It sways on ribs and a pelvis, climbs out of the vat, clatters to the ground. Once dead now alive, it's full of wishes. Opaque eyes, holes in the socket. The eyes fill with fire. First, a sizzle, the sound of voltage. Then a spark, a vomit of blue and pink lightning that zaps—the sound that you hear when you swat a fly. Behind the skeleton the vat furiously boils. Yellow-green smoke is floating from its jaws.

As Jasmin's head swoons, the smoke becomes feathers, and then mud, and then more skeletons rising from the boil. *Clatter-clatter-clatter.* Disremembering why they were dead, they plunge out of the vat's guile and begin a slow crawl from a joke or an irritation. No longer fragments they morph into humans as they near Jasmin, full-grown zombies reaching for answers.

Jasmin falls back, guides herself blind, hands groping the wall. She swirls to flee, but the walls are swaying and humping, the sound an explosion. *Clatter. Clatter. Ticky. Tock. Ticky. Tock.* She's near the doorway in the rectangle of the building when she sees him appearing, an apparition from the darkness of the circular room opposite. Knock-kneed legs, misshapen hands. Who can forget the leviathan head? His eyes are lights, a forensic gaze that burns. Jasmin trips over the pail to the sound of harsh laughter. The fall knocks her wind but something bionic guides her leap, her running. Behind, the sound of forever laughter.

Out the door, she races past a cluster of hedges, each shaped like the body part of a wild animal: the face of a warthog, the hind legs of a hyena, the mane of a lion, the horns of a topi. A star tree waves olive branches at her, branches that suddenly swoop and nearly crush her. She runs along a footpath that should lead to the children's garden but finds herself surrounded by foliage she's never seen. Trees whose leaves hug tight but open to scratch her as she whooshes past. Dog-eared sisal leaves that lift and hiss at her approach. The spike tree, each branch culminating into a ball of barbs that could shatter a skull. The many-eyed tree, all-over eyeballs moving as she goes. The torso tree that looks like the stump of a man, head and chest chopped off, just elephantiasis feet, giant-prune testes and a twisted phalange arching for the ground, but shoots in her direction, the eye of the penis opening.

A black crow, one green eye, one red eye, swoops from the torso, ambles, then hops in Jasmin's direction. She bursts with a cry away from the bad omen. She keeps running until her feet give. She sits under a monster tree, leaves resembling a bushy beast, limbs and head overwhelmed with a fur of green.

She sits there, unsure how long, and then tries to trace her way back. The air is balmy, her skin sticky, dirty as a curse. There's a new monument of a lion, slithering tongue out, his body that of a snake.

Tears burn in her eyes. A lump scorches her throat. But she has no cry. She's hopelessly lost. She's still wandering, disoriented, when she stumbles into Tolkien.

"We have a habit of meeting," he says.

She looks at him, so glad she has no words.

"I saw you running," he says.

"You followed me. Again. And found me with ease. After all, these gardens are your work."

"How can you tell?"

"Something the queen said."

He smiles, goes serious. "Earlier, you looked, what's the word? Unsettled. You looked upset as you ran—what was that about?"

"Guess," she says. "Atari!"

"You don't want to make an enemy of that one."

"I already have."

"I think you should come with me."

He guides her into the children's garden as though it were only meters away. He lifts the child-proof latch, lets Jasmin through first. She brushes against him, feels a rush to her cheeks. She walks swiftly toward the fat spider trees along the tiny lake. Now they stand, facing the floating lilies and water so clear you can see into its jaws, pebbles in its throat. Tolkien is way taller than her. His dawn-gray eyes are questioning.

"Now tell me. Exactly what happened."

She tells him about the vats, about the factory song and the swaying walls. Yellow-green smoke and then, ara k'davra—the golem with inanimate eyes that suddenly flash with lightning, then the golem becomes Atari. "He knows that I know about the vats," she says.

Tolkien considers her words. "Whatever it is that Atari is making, it must be hallucinogenic."

They are both silent for a moment.

She looks at him. "If you can go out into the sun any time—"

"Any time."

"What about the men who died? My husband?"

"Atari put a chemical in the men's supplement. In his future for Mafinga, men are a threat."

"But he trusts the teens—what's his name? Soho. And Junkie."

"The boys are a different generation: one Atari can manipulate."

"What happened to the animals, the trees? Supplements too?"

"Pollution in the soil, in the plants. It's the toxic waste from Atari's vats. It's doing something to Mafinga. Hopefully it's doing nothing to you."

His eyes through the hood appraise her crumpled Heidi dress with its short sleeves, its V-neck, its buttons racing all the way to her knees. A dress easy to throw over her head to wear, easy to throw off to undress. He's disrobing her with his eyes.

"Will you not?" she snaps. "Please." She walks away toward a gray goblin, standing feet asunder at the jaw of a cave. She races her fingers along the stony coolness of the pointy ears, traces teeth bared in a snarl, feels the hands—ready for naughtiness.

Again, Tolkien is too close. She arrives at the sandpit but, around him, a hammock is a perilous object to consider. She keeps walking and reaches the fat tree stump. He sits by her side. He takes her hand. She notices, *feels* the scars on his own. She smells him, a sweet almond smell. She stares at him.

"Jas . . ." a catch in his voice. His eyes are now a blue-green gray.

It's her turn to snatch his hand. She surveys the scars closely. "Take off the hood."

"Don't, Jas . . ."

"Take it off."

He lifts the hood, opens himself to her scrutiny.

She looks at his shock of white hair, his disfigured face. But it's him. The scent of old books, a sweet odor of vanilla. How had she missed it?

"Tolkien?" She's shaking, but her voice is sad. "The story maker. I should have guessed."

"I'm sorry."

"Do the children know?"

"Yes."

"Course, they do." She remembers the fist that held a marble that's a kaleidoscope of lights next to the chiffonier in the nursery, its gray skin the bark of an ancient tree. Godi was always good with his hands. Didn't he build the story machines. She remembers the children's secrecy.

"What's this then?"

"It keeps us safe," said Omar.

"Who gave it to you?"

"I tell. Me, Mamm!"

"No!" roared Omar.

"It's a secret. We can't say about him."

"The king?"

"Mama, we can't."

"How?" She refuses to believe it. "How is it that you're alive?"

"The queen saved me. Jas, she's kind."

"But how does she save a dead man?"

"I was never a good one for taking supplements. But I'd taken enough to cause harm. The queen visited Ujamaa Medico, found me barely alive."

"They told me you died."

"It kept you and me safe. The children too."

She's still for a moment. Then *slap*!

"All. This. Time! I thought—" She raises her hand to slap him again, but he grips her wrist, draws her to him, their faces so close.

"Solo," her voice is harsh, yet close to his lips.

"Solo is safe."

He pulls away. "There are—"

"There are what?"

"Complications."

"Dammit. I just wish—"

"A million times I wanted to tell you, send word. But I couldn't. You know I couldn't. Believe me, Jas. And then the king. My stories."

A surge of hope. "Baba Gambo?"

He shakes his head. "You saw it with your own eyes. No miracle will resurrect him. Atari is dangerous."

"The vats."

"I think he's experimenting to create an atmosphere that's perfect for an alien colony." He clutches her shoulders. "No one can know, least of all the children. You mustn't endanger them in any way."

"How dare you?"

"I will dare one more thing. Don't miss story time. Meet me after, at the stairs."

"Under the king's nose?"

"Where else is safe?"

9

Abebe slinks about in her mourning garb. Her peace for Jasmin is a poisoned chalice. She lays on the table a platter of chargrilled maize smeared with goat curd, a barbecue of wildmeat so gamy the room fills with an odor of copper and wet nut.

There's something ugly about the table in the servants' quarter, Jasmin is thinking. But the exact ugliness eludes her. Is it the color of its surface, a hue that is slate or is it lead? Perhaps it's the lump of its discrete presence in a room full of intent.

"It should be tender," Abebe is speaking of the meat. "I soaked it in buttermilk." She serves it up on a white porcelain plate decorated with baby pink flowers. Just then her face changes. "Stay away from Atari's plans. Don't imagine what he'll do if you become a threat. There's reality to what will happen to you."

Jasmin just about throws the plate at the woman. "Is there *poison* in this?"

"Maridadi warned me about you."

"What—is this the bitch club?"

"If I wanted you dead . . ." Abebe clicks her tongue.

"Then *you* eat it!" Jasmin leaps from the table.

* * *

The northeast tower and its coat of marble is petulant. The tents are in disarray, the train discarded. She feels uncalm in the nursery and

MAGE OF FOOLS · 125

it's spreading to the children. Mia is whimpering about something or nothing. Omar's is a stony sullenness.

"What's going on?" asks Jasmin.

"Nothing," says Omar.

"How about a story?"

"I don't know. . ." says Omar. And then: "A big people story?"

"There's this story of a dog that found a haunted hand—all flayed, wrist up," she coaxes.

"No, Mama."

Mia brightens. "Shiwo?"

"Tell us about the race between the clever little monkey and the lion cub," says Omar.

"Let's see," says Jasmin. She scrunches her face as if trying to pull out the story. "I don't know . . ."

The children tickle her until she "remembers."

"Okay, okay." She's laughing.

* * *

She waits at the stairs outside the king's chamber and its smell of devil whale shit. Godi steps out, shuts the door gently.

"Did anyone see you?"

"I don't think. Maybe . . . Abebe suspects something."

"There's a basement. It used to be a cellar. Follow me."

Down the winding staircase, down and down.

"Listen," says Jasmin. They freeze at a whisper, but there's no one there. Hearts pounding, they flatten against the stairs. Now there's someone. Abebe appears a floor below. She's holding a bundle of folded linen in both arms. She enters a room, takes her time to leave it. She pulls the door closed, doesn't glance their way when she departs. They wait more minutes than the situation commands, confirm that Abebe is truly gone.

Jasmin is at once aware of her entwinement with Godi, his excitement against her. She's both discomfited and elated by it.

She moves away awkwardly. They continue down the stairs in silence.

The cellar is a cold, dark room filled with a nose of sandalwood. Godi flicks on the lights. Two barrels stand on the hard cement floor. "Maize brew?"

"It's a mud shiraz."

"Let them eat cake." She looks at him.

Jasmin is aware of Godi, the perfect chemistry she feels. It doesn't need a glance or a touch to enliven her core. It's the thing that makes him metahuman, his effect on her. If he notices how she feels, her weakness to him, he doesn't show it.

"Come," he says. "There's a secret entrance to the mines here."

She follows him to the far side of the room. He stops by a wooden door with a bolt.

"Behind that door," he says. "Obey the sound of water."

"You aren't joking."

"I'm a resourceful man. I work with what I've got."

"I'm sure."

"A true sculptor shows his skill on crooked wood."

She smiles. "I could begin to like you. You've been listening to Mama Gambo and her wisdom."

"A lot has changed at Ujamaa Village since you left."

"It's only been days—please tell me Mama Gambo is safe."

"She's now running the shop at Ujamaa Village."

"Is that right." It's not a question. "What happened to that dog? Ulafi."

"Death by a thousand cuts. They cut out her head, put it between her knees. That's what happens to traitors."

"I'm guessing it wasn't the guards."

"There's only so many times you can poke a beehive with a dry stick."

Again, his face. So close. Her breathing rapid.

"The queen. There's something you should know." He doesn't meet her gaze.

"You're lovers?" she teases.

"Jas . . ."

"You're serious." Her shock is real. "It's you. Atari's hold on the queen." He doesn't answer. "First my husband. Now my children. Does she want to be me?"

"It's not like that."

"How is it then? Don't tell me it was part of her plan to kidnap me and my children under false pretenses to bring us to the castle."

"They're my children too."

"Now it's a custody battle?"

"Please, Jas. All I'm saying is that Maridadi has her own ambitions. Now listen to me."

"Why?"

"Because we must keep our minds to the task." He touches her arm. "And because Mama Gambo would say, 'The hunted reveals itself when the hunter gives up, packs the arrows and heads home.' We must stay focused, not give up."

"I'm listening."

"There are shafts in the mines. You could fall and injure yourself. Shall I come with you part way?"

She pulls from him. "Do you care?"

"I never stopped—"

Love is a pink light shimmering from the sky, mirrored on a frozen lake. Love is youth growing old as he courts you with a memory, and it's a track, a river, a bolt that opens to the sound of nostalgia. Love is finding something missing, and seeing it is a waterfall that's a language whose tongue is a panorama swollen with stars on the black velvet sky. Love is a mystic mountain rising from a crossing and it takes you to the deepest view of faraway nebulae.

Their hands are touching. This time he will kiss her.

But like a man who's taken, his focus shifts, brittle and clogged with weeds. "Someone's coming."

"Hurry! Get me out. Quick."

He fumbles with the bolt a forever time. Finally, it gives. The hefty door opens to a blast of wind. "This is it," says Godi. "Run!" He shoves her into darkness.

Suddenly she's afraid. The sound of the bolt slithering back. Jasmin clambers to her feet and runs.

ATARI

1

A womb is not for sleeping. It's for finishing transformation. Stealing the heart and brain of the weaker. Self-adjustments to flesh and bone. Atari's was an equilibrium of persistence and autocracy, amusement and subsistence inside the cavern of his mother's body. In a supreme world of advanced technology in Exomoon, who cared about X-rays? No one knew, nobody asked, about the vanishing twin.

Atari was always aware of himself, of his positioning with others, even from the womb. He quickly understood his brother's weakness and took advantage of it. First, he reached with tiny fingers and touched his brother's beating heart. The twin did not resist, which was good because Atari was hungry. He was very hungry.

He came out smiling in the arms of his nursemaid. Her name was Cancri. She carried him from an operating theater on a day that wore the yellow blaze of a sweltering sun, which was a day like any other in Exomoon and its extreme heat. They had to cut him out from his mother's womb, big as he was.

Later, as Cancri would explain to him, folk saw the leviathan head on his body and fell away in astonishment. As they thought back to their ancestors and the anomaly illuminated in the extraordinary child that the queen had borne, some suggested he was a curse. But Cancri knew he was a blessing, more so as the child's beam grew into a chuckle in her arms as she bore him with tenderness toward the nursery. She never saw the bones pushing out of his greedy body that had harvested his little brother. All she saw was a blessing.

Is a womb ever for sleeping?

King Gliese celebrated the birth of the prince with a feast in the palace. Exomooners attended, mostly out of curiosity. They were curious about the child, a first born who was an oddity, and about the palace because it was never opened to the public. They were intrigued by the silence of the house, now they could set foot in it, decipher its mystery.

Custom demanded that royals were revered at a distance. No one barged into their presence without invitation, and King Gliese and his queen, Ocean, never invited. They were an odd couple, cousins in fact, betrothed at infancy. Soon after the coronation, they took to the remoteness of the palace at the edge of the planet. Atari's mother was a domesticated woman who loathed servants but was compelled to pursue the services of a nursemaid to save her from fondling her own child.

The queen did not interfere with ruling, managed in weekly parchments to the king from the elders. Gliese did not appear before any council, never made any judgments in person. He simply signed. What the queen did was cook. Nimbly prepared platters of ghost potato, skinless and shaped in purple flowers; tuber yams, orange and yellow and full of sticky goodness; yazat tail sprouts, long stemmed with blue-green teardrop ends; dinosaur feet, flat-faced and drenched with sugar; succulent stones, each shaped like a pebble but it crumbled in the mouth in a watery goo.

At the birth of the child, upon the rare invitation by the king, Exomooners milled about the palace in their nakedness—of what use were garments in such relentless heat? They gasped at the luxury of the household, its lapis lazuli floors and jade bathrooms. They gaped at the onyx kitchen and its spinel faucets. The oratory of Atari's baptism and its moonstone pews. Its domed inner core, arched windows decorated with stained glass.

They took in the room's radiance, and traced with their fingers the shimmer of Alexandrite along the oratory's walls. They walked back and forth on the red velvet lining the center floor from the doorway to the emerald altar. Some even lay prostrate on the carpet, felt its opulence on their cheeks. They amazed at the wall behind the altar, and its embossing with blood-splattered carvings of sacrifices to the gods of the desert, of the sea, of marriage, of the dead. All manner of beasts—wendigos, chimera, manticores—lay sprawled with torn throats, gored chests, chopped heads, as a radiant god, sometimes wearing wings, posed with a foot atop each slain beast.

Exomooners would have climbed the peridot stairway to set eyes upon the golden canopy bed and its fantastical drapery, but Queen Ocean knew when a line was being crossed, and she could be very firm, as Atari came to understand.

As they gobbled winecup muffins, lilac and topped with white cream, and drank pink aloe whiskey, so tart that it was said to sharpen teeth, Exomooners were also searching for the king's name for his prince. It never wound up Head or Bones or Skull or Gargoyle or Golem, as some of them suggested, names the king pushed firmly back on. They seemed content with the king's choice of Atari, although they haggled a bit as a crowd, as was custom, but pulled back when the king turned his big round face and piercing gray eyes to them individually.

Atari's father was cold as winter, his lips straight as the stars of Orion. His mother bore warmth that was never directly focused toward Atari. It was only perchance that he caught her absent smile to his father. Hers was an oddity of soft lips on a sharp face. So, when she smiled, she became half pretty.

As if ashamed of their son, his parents kept Atari locked up in a nursery with Cancri. But there was one day that his father packed the family and its nursemaid into an egg shuttle, entered coordinates into the console and took them for an intergalactic ride to the Neutral Zone, away from Exomoon. There, they gazed at planets like Peridot and Tourmaline that shone brighter than jewelry, or the nameless one with burned-out stars in a cluster of thousands, an ancient planet that was older than life.

As for his mother, she never touched Atari until the day he created a sibling. The day that he did, she pulled Atari into her arms and, for the first time, he understood her scent.

It was a salty oasis.

2

His parents gave him to Cancri who raised him like her own in a closed room inside the palace. She had lived many years, and they showed on her face, but her diamond eyes were full of youth.

There was a difference about Cancri that told Atari she was not an Exomooner by birth. All he knew was that she was an old nursemaid with endless milk in her breast. He drank it and was filled with her presence, her spirit of calm. She enchanted him with her language, her stories in a foreign tongue that he all but understood. Awed him by her humble confidence as a servant in a household of detached parents. She touched his forehead, stroked his crown as he suckled. Sang him folklore about toddlers who played in a forest full of jubilant gods, and they bestowed upon the young ones gifts of wisdom and memory.

His gaze transfixed on her diamond eyes as she sang, on her age-withered face as if it were responsible for the beautiful sound that infused his being. From her throat came the sound of a brook bubbling over pebbles on its way to empty into a lake. The sound of a bee drinking nectar from a blonde dandelion capped with crimson pollen, winged with angel-white petals. The sound of quartz beads softly falling onto an aquamarine floor. His tiny palm clasped her big thumb. He blinked at the beauty of her ballad full of light and shadow, as it shifted with metaphors of seven sisters, a great big lightning bird and a moon full of superstition as it cartwheeled into the intersection of belief and the sea.

In the face of his parent's distraction from him, Atari understood Cancri's priority of one. He was the most important being in her life. He would never fall if she was within reach to catch him. She pocketed delicacies from his mother's kitchen and fed him marigold tarts and poppy cakes. There was no shortage of xeriscape plants in Exomoon, variants of wild blooms, cacti and succulents from which his mother could whip out a dessert.

Exomooners were vegetarian, but Atari had come from the womb with a craving for meat that Cancri understood. She took him on desert walks under the gargantuan brown and gray rings of the sizzler sky by day, or the icy cold of the tiny moons at night. She gently introduced him to desert fare such as bugs, gnats, wasps, ants, moths, beetles, spiders, termites and crickets that she watched him eat with interest, but never touched herself. Then, later, added diggers, locusts, hoppers, millipedes, centipedes, scorpions and snakes to his fare.

Despite his parent's aloofness, Atari stayed of a favorable disposition until the event that highlighted the sum of his individual importance to his parents, then culminated in an introduction to Doctor Quest.

* * *

He was six when he started hunting on his own. His first big kill was a thorny devil that gave sweet meat once he went past the spiked shell. One day he caught a baby-faced polecat. He stroked the small ears, the black mask face, the fat stomach, then he ate it. He knew he had matriculated well on the hunt when he caught the horned oryx and took it whole with its dark markings on its face and legs to Cancri. But much as he coaxed, she wouldn't partake in the meat. Cancri was everything. She was his culture, his way of being, his community. He had come to her with an offering, but she refused to take it.

For the first time in his life, he puckered up. His crying came out in hiccups that racked his chest, but only a solitary tear rolled down his cheek. Upon seeing him cry, Cancri who was sitting, leapt and tumbled, arms stretched to console him. It was a single tear, but it found its way to the ground. What it did next surprised them all, and Cancri stopped in astonishment. The tear that had slithered to the floor was no longer wet but a gelatinous blob. It was living thing, slimy as a toad, and it chirped.

Atari's mother rushed into the nursery, drawn by the odd sound of chirping in a generally silent household. Ocean gazed in horror at the jelly thing with a big nose and a mouth full of rubber teeth that futilely bit when she tried to touch it. His father hastened into the nursery, keen to understand the commotion, and was just in time to see the creature grow to the size of a child's fist. The pierce in his eyes pulled out a stammering explanation from Cancri in her foreign tongue, and it took a few attempts before his parents finally understood what had happened: Atari's tear had created a sibling.

It had never happened before. Exomooners were not renowned for powers of regeneration. This was a genetic anomaly, but it was a welcome one. Ocean got to her knees and took Atari into her arms. He nuzzled his head against his mother's chest but was confused by her elation. He understood it was something to do with his tear, and it took a while for him to link the happiness with the fact that he had produced a new child for his parents.

He'd never considered for a moment that they were trying for another child. He'd never imagined that he was not enough for them. Sure, he'd stumbled upon the sound of their mating, seen it too. His mother was bent over like a hog, his father right behind her, his bare rump moving. Gliese was making snarling noises and a pool of drool fell from his lip. His mother's noises were the call of a desert bird: *Epee. Eee. Eee.* The floor shook with tremors of an aftershock. His father's drool. His mother's *Epee. Eee. Eee.*

He'd never associated the mating with wanting babies. He'd

simply thought it was a thing that came with being grown up. He was convinced it was an ugly act he'd never partake in, no matter how grown up he became. He didn't like it and wouldn't do it, not if he had a choice, no. Later he wondered if the vigorousness of his parent's mating was responsible for the malformed twin—so weak in the womb, unable to survive on its own, Atari had to eat it.

His ecstatic parents immediately named the regenerate Gravity, watched over it where it cried in a cot that had once belonged to Atari. Cancri crushed a live centipede, sucked it into a syringe and fed the wailing thing as one would feed a wounded bird. But it cried as if in pain. They watched as it went into convulsions and burst into sudden slime all over the cot.

Atari's brother had lived only one day.

3

Despite Gravity's death, and the mournful ceremony in the oratory—himself, his parents and Cancri present—Atari could not help but notice his parent's new attitude, their sudden interest. His mother offered him poppy cakes dusted with sugar. His father who was mostly cool as frost took him and put him in the egg shuttle.

Atari looked forward to another intergalactic ride to the Neutral Zone. He asked his father why his mother or Cancri were not going on the trip with them. His father said nothing but looked at him with a gaze full of autumn. Even then, from height, Atari wished he had bidden Cancri goodbye. He peered down and saw her rushing out of the doorway of the palace, her gaze affixed to the skies. She waved at him with both hands. Now she was running, still gesturing up to him. He wondered why she was chasing in their direction—she'd never make it to Neutral Zone that way. He saw her fall to the ground, then she was a speck.

But it wasn't a faraway odyssey to see the dazzle of planets like gemstones from the vantage point of a neutral zone. It was a local ride to the laboratory of one Doctor Quest. The doctor's best work was right there, walking, potted or caged inside the lab. There was a tarantula hawk wasp with brittle bush for feet. A prickly pear with live beetles interwoven into the water-swollen leaves. A polecat that tightly wrapped itself in a cactus by day and unwrapped itself to prowl about its enclosure by night. Doctor Quest was a renowned genetic specialist.

Atari clung to his father's leg as he started to leave the lab. His father peeled off each of his son's finger and handed over Atari to Doctor Quest. As his father left the lab, the door slammed shut with a firmness that anyone else would have jumped at. Atari understood his predicament. His father had abandoned him as a subject at the mercy of the doctor's experiments.

Over days, or months, or years, the doctor watched Atari and the rest of the test subjects with curiosity. He monitored variations in diet, temperature, air, other elements. He carefully charted results, including each test subject's lifespan. Often, at the end of an experiment session, Atari was the remaining subject alive.

Doctor Quest was a tall, limby thing full of teeth. You never forgot the big smile on his face, even as he butchered you with a saw. He injected his subjects with a paralytic that stilled them but kept their mind alive to pain. The experiment would otherwise fail, reasoned the doctor.

"It will nout hurt one bit," he said in his grating voice that Atari would kill to forget. But it hurt each time, a lot. It hurt until it stopped hurting because the body conditioned itself to ignore pain after too much subjecting to it.

The only time Doctor Quest wasn't hurting his subjects was when he took a nap, the sleep of a thousand gods.

4

Atari's second sibling, Sirius, came from his blood. Doctor Quest drew a bowl of it with a fat needle, and that also hurt. Atari's blood began to clot and then form a creature with a flat head and snorkel lips. It vacuumed gnats when the doctor put them to its lips, but it refused to touch locusts. His parents took vigil over the incubator as Sirius grew to the size of a child's head. The thing croaked and croaked, then refused to feed even on gnats, and was dead in eleven hours.

Equator came from Atari's middle finger. Starry warts smeared half its face, the rest of its body covered in skin folds and more warts. It grew to the size of a newborn in seven hours and appeared to thrive on spiders and termites that it gobbled whole. But it too stopped eating and mewled as it died.

After the incident that begot Gravity, when the queen took Atari into her arms, she restrained herself from shows of physical affection when he created the rest of his siblings. She would quickly pat Atari on the head, as he lay strapped to a gurney, waiting for a chopped body part to regenerate, or to observe the new baby inside its incubator.

Doctor Quest took notes, observed how long it took to induce Atari's tears, drain his blood, slice off his finger . . . He inquired about Atari's pain threshold "on a scale of nout to googleplex," as he preferred to say, and each time noted Atari's refusal to answer. The doctor jotted how long it took for each butchered part to replace itself on Atari's body. He varied incubation conditions for each of Atari's siblings, watched as it developed and noted how long it lived, what sound it made before it died.

After Equator, his parents gave up on conventional naming and took to punctuation. Dash came from Atari's right hand. The sibling had compound eyes like those of a humungous fruit fly and grew to the size of a one-year-old in three hours. It gobbled diggers and scorpions, but it too stopped eating and groaned as it died.

The doctor sawed off Atari's left leg, and then his right, merged them in a vat, to create Colon. The sibling developed into something with a rock for a head, hammers for its hands. It pushed itself along in a snake slither on the floor and grew to the size of a three-year-old in an hour. It was a broody silent type that would not respond to Ocean's coos. But it pushed itself on the ground to swallow a lizard and bits of chopped up snake. When it stopped eating, everyone knew it would die. And it did.

Doctor Quest severed Atari in half to generate Hyphen. This one was fang toothed, bloated bodied, bulb-nosed and developed feet like a scythe. It had a shiny fish mouth as if someone had put lip gloss on it and a jaw full of razor teeth. It grew to equal Atari's full size in five seconds. It preferred polecat, the innards. It ripped the belly of a dead polecat with its teeth, pulled out and arranged the pancreas, the spleen, the kidney, even the heart. All remained untouched because the sibling only wanted the intestines, full of shit. It pulled them out of the carcass, ate them bite by bite. What more, this one could speak. Frankly, it roared. First its body ticked, then jerked, and random swear words tossed out of its mouth. It yelled: *Anus! Jerkoff! Twat!* But it started vomiting everything it had eaten, retching out its own innards, or perhaps they were those of the polecat. Then it made choking sounds as if someone was strangling it. Its legs trembled, just like a body in a hanging.

It too perished, and there was nothing anyone could do. The

doctor was at a loss—he'd tried everything. Atari's father scratched his head. His mother wept as though someone of import had died.

* * *

During his strapping on the gurney, in-between body chopping, Atari thought a lot about his parents. He could never come to terms with their greed for more children and sometimes wondered if things might have been different if his parents had embraced an ideology of the whole. The whole being the family as a unit. Gliese, Ocean, Atari (and Cancri) as a union. One, not three (or four, if he counted the nonblood bond of Cancri, who was also family). He worked out in his mind that the good of all was paramount to the desires of a few. The right attitude of mind would have cured his parents of their lust for more. How could they not see that Atari was integral to the equation?

He thought these things dispassionately. After years of experiment, nothing ever hurt, really, nothing ever could. He was resilient to pain, to feeling, and only one thing remained. He really wanted, in all earnest, that his parents abandon the quest for more children. Not from his body parts, no. Not from anything.

* * *

There was another girl in the lab, Doctor Quest's subject. Her name was Compass. She arrived days, or months, or years, after Atari's internment. He looked up when she arrived and impassively judged that she was bland as a stick. She seemed much eager to please, hands held in supplication like a mantis, until Doctor Quest restrained her onto a gurney. Unlike him, she had nobody to come and watch the outcomes of the experiments, someone like parents.

So, Atari watched instead.

Doctor Quest peeled the girl's skin in testing, studied her as she grew a new one. She couldn't cry out in discomfort at each flaying, how could she, paralyzed as she was? But Atari understood the drug was only for stillness, not for numbing. The girl could feel every inch of the procedure. The doctor peeled her feet up from the heels. He cut a seam and gently placed the small knife between skin and muscle, and pulled the skin back.

Sometimes Doctor Quest needed more knife to pare the skin from fatty tissue. He would repeat the process with the girl's hands, putting a seam in her palms, then carefully easing off skin around each finger. The doctor would continue to pull down, easing with the knife close to her flesh, until she was raw.

But within minutes of flesh gleaming like the inside of a fresh pumpkin, Compass would grow a new skin. Sometimes it was feathered like that of a desert bird, or haired like that of a hog, or scaled like that of a lizard, or an exoskeleton like that of a cockroach. But mostly it was Exomoon skin, slightly translucent with a pale green hue. Changing color like a chameleon, based on what she touched.

When the doctor took to his nap, right there in the lab, the girl tried to converse with Atari:

What's your name?

How long have you been here?

Do you have friends?

He never answered, but he wondered how Cancri was doing and wished she were there.

The stretchers were such that they adjusted for the strapped subject to sit, stand, kneel, lie sidewise. The beds were affixed with catheters and disposable pans for waste. Everything was an experiment. Even the washing. The doctor observed the subjects' reactions to different modes of cleansing. Mostly he dry-washed them with a sponge, soap and towel. The bright-green soap had a soft finish of curve leaf yucca, sickly sweet. Sometimes Doctor Quest escorted Atari and Compass to a shower that rained sizzling water. He watched as they stood alongside each other under the scalding downpour, too tired or too broken to care.

Every now, Doctor Quest allowed Atari and Compass out into the courtyard. But before then, he injected them with a sedative so they were about right to take in and blink at the light through the sunroof, too weak to escape. They would loll about with stupid smiles, ecstatic at their freedom from straps. Sometimes they accidentally touched or fell into each other in their stupor. Doctor Quest took notes.

Compass was developing, her chest coning into perfect-shaped breasts. Atari noticed the breasts. But he only observed them as one would a different colored locust. His memory of breasts was of fragrant milk that reminded him of tiger tooth aloe. Of Cancri, as she sang him folklore. He wondered if his mother and Compass could produce milk, let alone sing.

5

One day Doctor Quest wheeled in a new subject.

Atari felt her presence. Her fear, her pain. Only one other held such a metaphysical bond with him and that was his former nurse-maid, the alien with a presence, a divine vocalist who bonded souls with Atari when she sang.

This silent song told of petals and violins and a place called home. It was a racing river flowing into a grotto, echoing off the walls in a pattern of emerald-green shimmer as a flamed phoenix circled overhead. She opened her mouth one last time and released a soundless story of godless beasts shaped in punctuation, but the period was clashing swords with the question mark. At an exclamation point, two semicolons braced into an apostrophe that shot ellipses of fire, dashing like dragons and there was no parenthesis, clarity or conviction in the underside of wings. She closed her mouth one last time and he felt the truth of brackets, how enclosing they were, and he wondered what was inside the punctuation that remained essential to her narrative. Just then a whisper of her soul escaped. It tasted of rain and summer, suncups and dandelions in desert-yellow distinction.

But such gifts were not the kind developed in a lab. When Doctor Quest chopped, the subject did not heal. Atari felt her kindness as she diminished. Her final gift was a warm spirit and it flew toward him, a prayer for him, for his strength. Then he felt her let go, and she didn't resist the going. He felt her peace before she went cold.

Doctor Quest piled her limb by limb, and finally head, into a disposal bin and wheeled it away.

6

After the death of Hyphen, his parents went quiet for a while, never coming to visit. Now that he'd been severed in half, and grew back, Atari wondered what more they might try. What was left was to butcher the rest of him and try to regenerate something big. But he knew, his parents knew, the doctor knew, that the larger the sibling grew, the shorter it lived. Gliese and Ocean were desperate for a child at Atari's cost, at any cost.

What was there to stop them from an ultimate sacrifice?

Atari resigned himself to fate and imagined each day as his last. If he were to perish, he asked himself, what would he miss the most? He thought long and hard, and occasionally thought of poppy cakes or marigold tarts. Without Cancri, the answer right then was too difficult. He was born to wealth, but it never felt like privilege. If he lived to become ruler, he would strip everyone to a simple life, perhaps in a desert full of stars, and encourage them to eat meat. But it was questionable that he would live.

One day without warning, his face still winter, his father entered the lab. Atari wondered where dying would take him. He was not afraid of pain—he'd endured too much of it to matter. But he was curious about the afterlife. Would he meet his siblings? He didn't want that.

He was thinking all this, as his father first nodded at Doctor Quest, even at Compass. To Atari's surprise, his father leaned and unstrapped Atari from the stretcher. He touched him with cold hands, unplucked the catheter and went on to give his son a dry wash. Atari's legs were shaky when he put them to the floor. His father guided him with an arm on the shoulder, and then by hand as Atari regained strength in that instant. Gliese took Atari, now a young man, and helped him into the egg shuttle.

Atari blinked as his father entered the coordinates for home.

That is how Atari found himself, not dead, but soaring back home to the palace, to become a son again. In his hands he clasped a souvenir of history now transformed, a strange request that even Doctor Quest was taken aback at, but it was a request that the doctor had been too astonished, and too indebted, to refuse. The souvenir was a dose-filled vial of the paralytic and a syringe. Atari needed it to remember where he had come from, what he had endured, and the magnitude of his survival.

It appeared that, inside their detachment, there was hope for Gliese and Ocean. They were beginning to see reason. It appeared that, finally, after much unsuccessful trying for a child through their son's regenerative gift, they had chosen the right path that meant a new chapter for Atari.

But home was lacking without Cancri. Atari felt a stranger in the mute chorus of his parent's great hall and its amethyst walls that stayed silent even when the handful of guests came to visit. He felt alone. Others to him were dots he saw from the height of a shuttle to or from somewhere. Others were 'randoms' he bumped into along the corridors of the palace as they hastily departed with a parchment to or from the king. Others were his father, his mother, Cancri—who was no longer in existence, Doctor Quest, Compass. Atari didn't know many *others*.

Perhaps sensing Atari's emptiness, and to make up for years of amiss, Gliese escorted Atari into the egg and entered familiar coordinates that flew them all the way to gaze at beautiful planets from the vantage point of Neutral Zone. Gliese handed Atari a superscope and pointed out Pegasi, the world an eyeball with a crimson pupil that glowed.

"That there is Neptune," he said, and Atari gazed at the planet's velvet blue surface full of ice. "And that is Enceladus." It was ice-crusted, a beautiful dream. From afar Atari thought it looked like a desert bird's egg.

"That's the Hat-Planet," pointed Gliese. "It rains purple amethyst and blue turquoise."

Atari was struck by its beauty, and was still awed when his father pointed out Earth. "It's a wet planet full of lakes and oceans." Gliese laughed, "People there are a bit backward."

The sound of his father's laughter startled Atari who had never heard it. It was the cough of a polecat, or the sound Atari's last sibling made as it choked and died.

Gliese went serious. He opened his palm and gave Atari a dull stone. "Rub it," he said.

Atari rubbed, and the stone shone.

"Bite it," said his father.

Astonished, Atari bit and offered the stone back to his father, who also took a bite.

They stood, tourists in the Neutral Zone, two comrades sharing a cantata of the nebulae as they faced the galaxy. The drug effect was not a rush, but it was total. Atari felt dizzy and delirious all at once, then a surge of adrenaline that lifted him off the ground. He felt within, yet without, at one—yet pulled out of himself as he slowly began to turn.

Through the haze, from the edge of his eye, he saw his father also lift, slowly turn on air, and his entire body was luminous like a rare moon in a glow integral to the rapture. As gaiety overtook him, Atari's head filled with lilac and white petals that burst into song. Somewhere in a stanza of the intergalactic paean, his father said, "Mafinite," through the haze. "It grows on the wet planet."

Atari nodded, laughed, despite the obscurity of his father's words, the potential allegory in them. All that mattered was the equal sharing of pleasure on some remote dot in that gigantic space, standing with this father who was no longer a stranger to him.

They stayed there for hours, wrapped in the dull emptiness of a neutral zone, right there in the gut of the cosmos. They were surrounded by the beauty of planets hundreds of light years away. Atari spread his arms, threw back his head. He felt at one with nature, with the universe. He felt kinship and beyond. He felt warmth as radiant as the one he'd felt with Cancri.

But he was careful not to cry his joy, lest some unborn sibling took ownership of his tears and squirmed without distinction, a gelatinous predator, and borrowed into his life to make him an abstraction.

7

On the way back home in the shuttle, Atari said to his father, "Teach me how to fly."

Gliese leaned forward, opened a map of the galaxy on the dashboard. "It's easy," he said. "Technology for dummies. You touch a location and it gives you the coordinates."

Atari looked at Mercury, Saturn, Uranus, Wasp-12b, GJ-504b, Earth, Jupiter . . . so many planets, all charted with coordinates on a map.

As days went by, Atari felt closer to his father. He thought for days of that moment of giddiness that was also an anchor, a shared moment of comrades in a void. He savored the deliriousness, the melody in his head, remembering how their bodies floated off the ground. He wanted to do it again.

He wondered how his father had obtained the mafinite. One day he stole into the shuttle, studied its map closely. His father had hand-marked Earth with a pen, right there, a blue marble, swirls of cloud on it, speckled with greens, yellows and whites. But all Atari wanted was to go to Neutral Zone, not Earth, with his father.

Gliese bode his time, not once tossing the invitation Atari so yearned, or whipping out that magic stone and offering a bite of it in a moment of camaraderie, a sharing of the drug with his son. One evening at the dinner table, as they ate red pancakes served with baked cactus pie, and drank golden barrel wine, Atari opened his mouth to broach the delicate but important matter. The gaze of complete fondness that his mother threw in his direction shut him up.

"We're pregnant," she gasped.

"Yes. Your mother and I are pregnant," said his father.

Atari looked at them in disappointment. The word disappointment could not begin to describe what went through him. His parents had slaughtered his trust. Family was community, but his parents had first disrespected it in their harvesting of his body for their individual gain. And now this.

What purpose did other siblings serve to Atari than to introduce disorder into an established sociodynamic? After the botched-up prototypes of siblings that had grown from his tears, his blood, his fingers, his legs, his torso, he'd hoped, really hoped, that his parents had abandoned the idea of improving a family that was the perfect size at three.

He quietly rose from the table. Alone in his room, a lone tear rolled down his face. He snatched it in his fist, crushed it, before it could transform.

* * *

That night, Atari stood outside their bedroom. Head in his hands, he leaned against the blue sapphire balustrade. He listened with detachment to the animal sounds of his parent's mating. His mother's cries of a desert bird: *Epee. Eee. Eee.* The floor shaking with tremors in an aftershock. He waited until the trumpet finish of their snoring told him they had reached the stage of deep sleep.

Inside his parent's bedroom with its canopy bed and fantastical drapery made of silk, his father's drool-licked face wore big round certainty, even in sleep. His mother's hand was sprawled across Gliese's chest, her naked lips in a half-smile on the sharp face that had given Atari nothing that contained warmth, except for poppy cakes and marigold tarts.

He stabbed each of them with the paralytic, first his father, then his mother, in that order. He used a bread knife on his mother. Her eyes flew open too late. He sliced through her neck as his father, now awake but immobile, watched. Atari put his lips to his father's frosty skin, touched his body. He wondered how different things might have been if only his father had shown a little more affection. Patted Atari's head, stroked his face, held his hand in the same way as he had done the day he unstrapped him from the lab and walked him into the shuttle to take back home his son. Atari remembered Cancri, who sang songs that were flowers, jewels and waterfalls. Cancri, who told stories of gods that were kind and full of mercy, and they played with children. Cancri, wheeled in, in a stretcher, wheeled out, in pieces in a bin.

Atari opened his mouth and took a bite. His father tasted a bit like a polecat, just less hairy and more gamey. Atari's mouth filled with a burst of copper. As his father looked at him with eyes that begged, the rest of his body rendered immobile, Atari took another mouthful of the cold, lean steak. He gorged himself chomp by chomp, until he could eat no more.

* * *

As his parents lay dying, Atari turned the bedroom inside out. He yanked the wall-mounted mirror gilded in gold, but there was no safe behind it. He tore side drawers next to the bed. Kicked apart an antique chiffonier and its headboard of the rarest wood. Ripped deluxe goose pillows soaked with his parent's blood. He ran down the peridot stairways, threw asunder recliner sofas and portraits of his father's lineage through eons mapped on the tourmaline walls in the great hall. There was not a speck of mafinite, the drug that had made him fly without wings, that had transformed his body to the radiance of a rare moon.

He threw open the door, stood in the oratory and its moonstone pews. Its domed inner core, arched windows decorated with stained glass, issued a silent warning or a curse. He gazed at the shimmer of Alexandrite along the walls, at the crimson velvet lining the center floor from the doorway to the emerald altar, at the wall behind the altar embossed with blood-splattered carvings of sacrifices to the gods of the desert, of the sea, of the dead. Radiant gods posed with a foot atop all manner of slain beasts—wendigos, chimera, manticores.

Right there as he sought meaning in this strange oratory that fit perfectly, yet didn't, the sky in the room was first full of ash and then stars. The air transformed into a shimmering sea-blue haze infiltrated by rays of a strong, pink sun. White baby stars dazzled the constellation pregnant with unborn planets. He felt out of place in this out of body experience inside an oratory full of mythology. He did not belong here. The heatless sun commanded half the room in a cherry haze. The other half flickered with the ethereal sea and its slow bubble of white tide.

He waited the following day, close to Doctor Quest's nap. He rode the shuttle to the lab. There he was, the doctor, sprawled on a gurney, snoring like a beast. Atari injected him with the paralytic and then took out a saw. As the doctor's eyes opened in drowsy sleep, Atari decided he wasn't fond of Doctor Quest's face.

Compass brightened at his approach.

"I knew you'd save me," she whispered.

Having spent years locked up together in a lab he wasn't astonished at her look of gratitude. But he wasn't expecting that warmth in her eyes, something that reminded him of the way Cancri had looked at him.

"Untie me," she smiled. "Help me off the stretcher."

He looked at her for a long time, then carefully picked a knife. He flayed her as he'd seen Doctor Quest do, feet up from the soles. Her silent tears . . . the muscle paralytic fully working. When she was raw, before her new skin could grow, he put his hands to her head and turned it from its neck. Not much point in leaving her alive strapped on the gurney.

He returned to the egg shuttle, set its coordinates for the wet planet.

8

But Earth was not a wet planet.

Not in the way he'd imagined. The egg shuttle crashed into a red-rock monolith, creating a gorge that crumbled with stone. Atari crawled out of the gullet, and reached for a ledge to hoist himself up. He was astonished to see what he held.

It was mafinite.

He couldn't believe his good fortune. He admired his father for a moment, marveling at how Gliese knew to set on the galactic map exact coordinates that would take him straight to the source of mafinite, tucked away in the great big marble and its white swirls. Earth. The blue was meant to be water—but there was none here.

Atari shook his father from his head, wondered what now. He'd need help to retrieve the shuttle from the gorge. He hoped the vessel was undamaged—hadn't his father said that Earth's technology was a bit backward?

Atari's knowledge of other people was limited to what he'd experienced with his parents, with Cancri, with Doctor Quest, with Compass, so he didn't know how to deal with the fully clothed woman he'd clearly frightened. She peered at him from the top of the gorge.

"Take me to your leader," he tried.

He was surprised that she understood, because she turned and took to her heels in the direction of the wind. He ran after her, but she ran harder as if being chased by griffins. He followed her past trees like sticks, their branches all arms asunder. She ran up a hill to a compound at its crown. She skidded into what appeared to be a royal court and, breathless, pointed at him to the people.

Indeed, the woman had led him to the king and his queen—they wore crowns.

Atari, naked and alien, stepped into the hall. All eyes turned on him. Stared at his skin, slightly translucent with a pale green hue, changing color like a chameleon's. He felt unease. He was uncomfortable with others.

But he noticed something about the queen. Something that reminded him of Cancri—perhaps it was her quiet strength. She was holding a sick child that was at first squirming and squealing, then it slumped and went silent.

Atari walked to the queen and eased the baby from her arms. She let him take it.

The rest was history.

* * *

What Earth people didn't understand was that it was one thing to heal a dying prince by letting him suckle the sweat-filled finger of someone with regenerative powers like Atari. It was another to anticipate that the miracle would continue in a frail human body that had a weak liver and bad kidneys.

For years, Atari had resuscitated the prince who was now king with his alien body fluids: a lick of sweat, a drip of urine, a spatula of blood. Now King Magu's kidneys were rejecting the cumulative effects of whatever it was that powered Atari's body to regenerate. And it was just as well, because Atari had no tolerance for men. One day, after he'd rid Mafinga of its king, he might have use of the queen. Not for procreation, that was certain. The look of love he'd rejected from Compass before he flayed her had helped to affirm his asexuality. He had a fervent distaste for intimacy, for mating. He'd seen and heard enough of how his parents did it, witnessed how it stripped them of glory, reduced them to wilderness, to know there was nothing royal about the act.

He remembered, as a child before the laboratory, how one day he was hunting when he came upon two pixie frogs by a pond. The male was the size of two thorny devils, the female the size of three. The male was locked onto the back of the female, the whole mucus green and white of him slowly breathing, the small striped eyes on its green slimy body staring straight at Atari. He observed how, soon after the mating, the female turned on its male, first bit and then incapacitated it with venom. Atari watched in fascination as the female stretched its mouth to gobble every slimy morsel of the male's pregnant body and its buttery underside.

Much like that female pixie frog's distrust of the male, Atari distrusted males. They had potential to transform and turn into brothers. His punishments for the defiant males, like Baba Gambo, were personal and harsh. In the end, he exterminated them swiftly and decisively with deadly intent. As for women . . . They were gnats: other than try to create children you didn't want, what serious harm could they do? Ridding Mafinga of the male populace solved that problem.

And now Atari's experimentation of an ideology of the whole was moving in the right direction. The secret was to make people hollow inside, make them forget. You discovered that, once dead inside, including in the head, they blindly followed. Knowledge, such as that of Doctor Quest, was an enemy of the people.

Despite his ban on readers, the supplements to make them forget, Atari knew that Earth people mistrusted him, first and foremost for being an alien. He needed Queen Sheeba for when the king died. With her quiet strength like Cancri's, she was one the people of Mafinga might trust. Whatever people thought, Atari was not interested in a coup d'état; he had no desire to reign. What he wanted was unlimited access to the mafinite, and people to mine it.

The king's mine was nearly exhausted. Only Atari knew there

were fresh supplies of the magic stone at Red Rock. What he needed from Queen Sheeba was leverage. And he found it in the scar-faced Einstein who created the story machines and an antidote against the chemicals that had poisoned the soil. *That* was an accident. Atari was trying to recreate a habitat to grow the wild blooms, cacti and succulents of Exomoon. But none of them grew. Not the ghost potatoes, tuber yams, yazat tails or dinosaur feet. Instead, the chemical had killed Mafinga's plants and animals.

How he missed the food of his mother's kitchen. Food shaped in a flower, or orange and yellow and full of sticky goodness. Food molded in a pebble but crumbled in the mouth. He'd never learned to make poppy cakes, winecup muffins or marigold tarts. He'd tried instructing Abebe, who could never be Cancri, not even a homunculus version of his former nursemaid. The food Abebe produced was a deathstalker that tasted like rock hopper poop.

Many times, he'd considered setting the shuttle coordinates back for Exomoon to get ingredients, but he'd slain the king and queen; who would want to come back with him as a cook? No, he had no more use of the egg shuttle, he'd donated it to Mafinga. And there was plenty of meat in this world, enough humans such as Baba Gambo to harvest, and they stewed well with mafinite in the vat.

One day in a new curiosity, Atari took a razor and sliced off his little finger, nail upward. He snatched the squirm before it fully formed into a sibling, drowned it in a pail of the vat's simmering liquid. The creature squeaked as it died, a melt into the broth. Atari scooped some with a ladle and let it cool. He licked a drop with the tip of his tongue, then committed to a swallow. It was a waltz of the gods. The high he experienced was a flowing rollercoaster that spiraled in and out of galaxies.

The finger grew back. The experience told Atari that, if needed, he could be his own supply of endless meat. But he didn't need to go to such extremes, because he knew one thing more. There was uranium at Red Rock. He'd personally overseen the sample testing.

The trio of humans he'd borrowed from the king's mines to drill out samples was long molten in his vat, brewed as sustenance and rapture. Soon, there'd be mass transportation of people to service the new mines. And that meant a big harvest, because casualties were unavoidable.

Red Rock was a killing field.

THE RESISTANCE

1

Jasmin falls into the darkness of the cave. Her mind is blank for a moment, all language gone except for full stops and commas. The punctuation morphs into rocs, krakens and manticores. Run. Run. Jasmin is running. Run, Jasmin run, fast, faster.

The beasts in her head make her think of sentences that have a pause and an ending. Nothing is ambiguous in each punctuation, everything is ominous.

Run. Run.

The roc breathes close to Jasmin's ear, the message in its whisper clear as a curse: *A scorpion moves quickly in a warm dark place, and the toxins of its stinger bring numbness, tingling or death.*

Run, run.

With each comma and full stop, Jasmin is unsure of her footing. She staggers and spills to the ground, hands and legs everywhere. The kraken uses tentacles to cling to Jasmin's head. Its limbs glide down the back of her neck as it chatters into her ear: *A rat squeaks and hisses, and then it bites. The bite isn't serious, but it infects you with fever and the bacteria can cause gangrene.*

Jasmin shoots to her feet and runs. Run, run, run, run.

But the manticore is run, run, running with her. It hisses its news, the meaning somber as doom: *A snake pushes off the surface and moves all wavy. It strikes from any posture and, if coiled, whips its head to attack across distance.*

Runrunrunrunrunrunrun.

Her memory is refilling with words—this time of author Maddison in a narration about fear:

There are many levels of darkness—first, there's darkness like a magazine announcing the end of the world that needs to lose you to find you. Nothing has changed but everything is churning, faster, faster, and you have no place in it. Then there's darkness like a monstrous trunk, and it siphons you into a great big throat, down to a large intestine full of goblins with teeth. At the pinnacle of all darkness is the one that's an assault by all your phobias, and it is darkness like a thought or a memory, a childhood home with black crows posed along the ledge, lining the window like stiffs. But the crows are not dead—they have ruby in their eyes, and their stare is shifting, many lies and facts in each gaze. It begins to drizzle meat from the sky, and the bits of mince cling as they fall, forming the shape of carrion that gets bigger and bigger as it falls, and the carrion is you.

Run, Jasmin, run. Down, down, down in the dark.

She has a phobia and it is one of many. This fear is not about krakens or manticores. It is a craven terror of rats and snakes. And the terror is forming questions about snakes: which ones will Jasmin encounter? A puff adder with its stumpy appearance, triangulated head, skin the color of coral? A beautiful assassin, sluggish as it moves in a straight line like a caterpillar. But it's no caterpillar when it listens to the vibrations of your footsteps, waits unseen, inflates and hisses as it strikes with a bite whose agony you'll live to remember.

Will it be a boomslang that lies in wait, motionless like a twig, camouflaged to the color of any surface? You'll think it part of the landscape before it breaks off the surface with an attack that leaves you hemorrhaging, and you just might die. What if it's a viper, coiled in a spotted ribbon, vertical pupils staring with keenness at only you? This snake is sensitive to infrared—it understands your heat image, the pulse of your warm-blooded dread. Its keeled scales shift before you see them, and you're still blind to the fangs as they hit.

Even yet, it could be a spitting cobra that sways in response to a snake charmer's music, slow to strike, but it will strike. The snake lifts off the ground, swells neck to rib and thrusts its grooved fangs with a tiny bite that will paralyze you. But none of these compares to the black mamba with its body the color of charcoal, its underside the color of poisoned milk. Button eyes filled with night to survey you, a mouth lined with ebony, waiting. The creature slithers at speed, rears up a flattened hood. Two drops of its venom will stop your beating heart.

Runrunrunrunrunrunrun.

Finally, Jasmin is out of wind. She pauses, gathers herself. Steels herself from the creep of irrational panic. She doesn't need a torch to see, her eyes are aglow and she hasn't seen any snakes. She must sharpen her will to survive. She must slaughter her fear.

It's then that she sees the stalactites. They're hanging like sword chandeliers from the cavern. Her night vision, eyes acquainted to darkness, picks out the multicolored ones from the white ones and the yellow-brown ones. She walks slowly, leaving the crystalized formations behind. She takes in the setting around her. The air is tepid but clean.

She keeps walking until she reaches a cage door with a steel ladder. She pulls open the latch, steps into the narrow shaft. She reaches with both hands, levels herself onto the ladder. Her shoes are not right, they're flat-soled and slippery.

Drip, drip, the walls around her are wet. Drip, drip, now her face is wet. Drip onto her sleeves. Drip onto her gown. She couldn't be near a water table, too high isn't it? She's poorly dressed in the stupid Heidi dress that clings. Down one rung, down. Such conditions: how is it that Solo has not caught pneumonia from this horrid place?

Jasmin tries but fails to keep her mind away from her phobia of going up or down a height. The dread is in her throat, each motion a freeze. She must coax the muscles to move. And how is she to forget her fear of closed spaces? The space is a coffin, the width of a person. One slip off the wet rung, and she might be grave material. She remembers the proverb: *Little by little* . . . soon she'll arrive to something, somewhere.

Down one rung, down. She reaches a platform, but there's another ladder. More platforms, more ladders. Acid is building in her muscles.

And with ebbed terror comes a gnawing hunger. It's a claw in her stomach. She remembers the food she threw at Abebe, can taste the chargrilled maize smeared with goat curd. Wild meat so gamy, it oozed an enticing aroma of copper and nut drenched in buttermilk.

Another platform, another ladder. Can she go one step more? One more.

Just as she thinks she really couldn't climb any further down, she steps to the last platform. A musty earth smell surrounds her. Water drip, drip, drips. The place is still a coffin. Jasmin is standing on the platform, nowhere to go but up. It's a dead end.

With a sob, she starts the slow climb back up.

2

Jasmin reaches the last ladder to the top. She heaves herself onto firm ground. Retraces her steps in the cavern. Arrives at a fork, hesitates. *Eeny meeny*—she chooses a direction at a gamble. Another dead end. She turns, panic in her throat.

She walks back toward the fork, takes the opposite direction, but it too—a rocky uneven surface—is a dead end. She mentally walks the route, navigating in her head how she got there, the path from the castle. If she faces this way, the stalactites to the back of her, she must be looking toward the cellar.

But everything is wrong.

It's a maze when she tries it, barricades everywhere. Here is a nothing wall. Here's a pile of rock. She thinks of her children. Mia and her pigtailed cornrows, her natural scent of orange or lemon. Omar and his burst of curls, his tea-colored skin soft as a baby's. She'd give anything to clasp them one more time. They're all the strength she needs right now.

She spies another entrance, walks carefully toward it. She pulls herself at the last minute from stepping into the maw of a gaping hole. It's a wide, open shaft. She's lost, hopelessly lost, and being lost in this world is a deadly roulette.

Do you care?

I never stopped—

She wishes Godi was here. She should have taken his offer to go with her part way. She wishes that, by now, he fully understands the treachery of the mines, realizes Jasmin's foolishness and plight, and will come to her aid.

Godi is not coming.

In the crest of Jasmin's despair, she hears the sounds. Squeaks, hisses, chatters. Movement, something dragging itself toward or away from her. She tries so very hard not to think of rats and snakes. Godi—why isn't he here for her?

Because he's occupied with the king, telling the dying fool stories to keep him alive. He's preoccupied with the queen, doing . . . what? How could he forget the touch of his lips on Jasmin's skin, her cry of pleasure as he found her, how time both stopped and raced until it erupted in a panorama of colors? Jasmin wonders what the queen looks like, sounds like, when she's wrapped in Godi's arms.

Her thoughts are murderous when she notices the breeze. The air is good—surely, she must be close to the castle. She hears footsteps. Godi. About bloody time. Unable to restrain herself, she calls in elation, "Hello, I'm here."

The walls answer: *Hello, ello, lo.*

She calls out again and the walls echo: *Hello, ello, lo.*

And then a real voice: "Hello."

The walls echo it: *Hello, ello, lo.*

Jasmin leaps with new strength. "Godi. I'm here!"

Here, here, here.

He's running toward her.

She's running toward him. "I'm here!"

Here, here, here.

Then the sound of laughter. Jasmin stops.

She sees the dance of the approaching torchlight, then the tall shape of a woman curved in all the right places. It's Maridadi.

"Little mouse. I knew I'd find you."

Jasmin stares at her, too stunned to move.

"Think of all the things I'm going to do to you, little mouse."

"How did you know I was here?" Jasmin tries to keep her voice steady. Reason with the enemy, she's telling herself. The torchlight is right on her face.

"Abebe kept a keen eye on you, didn't she now?"

"She had the means. She could have killed me. All that food."

Maridadi laughs. "And ruin the fun?"

They stare at each other. Then Jasmin swirls and runs. The echoes of her running, the stampede of Maridadi's chase.

Maridadi's laughter. "Run, run, little mouse."

Jasmin suddenly stops, whirls. She catches Maridadi's hand, pulls her forward, trips her with a foot. Jasmin moves backward as Maridadi recovers her breath. "That's how it is?" says the guard. "Little mouse will fight. I'll enjoy that."

Jasmin again runs. Maridadi is gaining on her. Jasmin hears, "Shit," then a crash, the guard's fall, accompanied by a clatter of the torch and the light dies.

Maridadi climbs to her feet. Her arms are out, she's pawing the air, feeling her way.

Jasmin realizes Maridadi can't see well in the dark. The privileged eyes of a guard are unaccustomed to the kind of darkness the rest of Mafinga, the unprivileged ones, must endure.

"Come on, little mouse," Maridadi is calling. "You know you can't get away."

Quietly, holding her breath, Jasmin looks around, studies the space she must maneuver. Then she sees it, lets out her breath. "Here," she calls. "Come get me."

Maridadi's run is blind. She stamps with her boots toward Jasmin at speed.

Jasmin flattens herself against the cavern's wall. Maridadi whooshes past, plunges into the wide, open shaft. Her scream is forever, then a soft thud like the landing of a sack of potatoes and the banshee sound cuts.

Jasmin sits in the horrible silence for a moment, then she's violently sick. Her empty stomach retches out water and air, each heave a torment to her ribs. She's crying and laughing, then a drum enters her head. She crawls away from the vomit, away, away from the maw, as if Maridadi might suddenly climb out of the shaft and renew the chase.

Jasmin sits against the wall, leans her full weight on it, pulls her knees, cradles her head in her arms. It feels heavy, the drums multiplied to a thousand and still pounding. What more, her forehead is on fire. But she must keep moving. She rises on wobbly knees. Uses the wall to guide her. Godi is never coming to help. She must find Solo.

Her walk is weak. The authors, deep in her subconscious, talk their encouragement. Flaubeatrice. Temper. Maddison. Shellon. Harper. Mandoza. Gladwell. They remind her of courage, promise, freedom, love, identity. She arranges their names in alphabetical order. Flaubeatrice. Gladwell. Harper. Mandoza. Maddison. Shellon. Temper. She arranges the themes of their language alphabetically, goes through the words over and over to grasp their strength. Courage. Freedom. Love. Identity. Promise.

The words are Jasmin's silver bullets, her immutable vests. One step more, one more, she whispers. She doesn't know how long she must walk. She just keeps moving until—suddenly—she hears the soft sound of water coming or going.

She imagines a river swollen by a tide, bloated waters washing in indignation to drown her logic of surviving. She remembers her children's hair, one's long braids, the other's tight curls. Each truth embroiders her memory with a fine silk that rustles to a perfection of the unforgotten. She longs to walk naked on butterfly milkweed under a safe and calming sun, lift her face to its fresh yellow rays full of incandescence that never blisters or haunts.

She seeks to find connection in her disconnection. She's made sacrifices. A lot of things have happened outside her own doing but, so far, she's kept her head, her spirit. Something called fate put her in the castle. There, even as a servant, she never faltered. She made crucial discoveries that could save Mafinga.

And this choice is hers. To leave the children, reach the resistance. Tell them about the sun, about the king, about Atari's growing threat. One step more, one more. She deserves more. She deserves a good ending.

The fever's escalation hits without warning. Jasmin keels to the ground. She curls into herself, teeth chattering with cold, then a burst of heat assaults her body. At the rage of her delirium, her mouth tasting of ash, she feels herself sink into the jaws of a great black serpent.

"Help," she whispers.

The sound of rushing feet.

3

She's in and out of consciousness. Somewhere in the haze, the sound of a bell. Hands. At one point someone is dragging her. She welcomes the blackness.

Movement. Voices. She opens her eyes. Warm hands, a rain of kisses on her face. "Jazzie. Jazzie." Solo swims into focus.

Jasmin touches the unwashed braids. "It's you," she croaks. "Really you."

She's lying on a makeshift bed in a dimly lit place. It's a cave and not a cave. A cow moos. There's a smell of chicken poop. How is this a cave? "Where am I?"

"You imbecile," says Solo. "What were you thinking?"

"I got lost," whispers Jasmin.

A chameleon looks in all directions, and then it moves, says Mama Gambo.

"I was looking, but I still got lost. And Maridadi—"

"Hush. You're safe now."

"Where am I?"

"In our camp, and it's a good one. You're safe, Jazzie." The sound of water coming and going. "It's natural groundwater, flows out into a fresh creek."

Jasmin smiles. *No matter how full the river, it still wants to grow,* says Mama Gambo.

"We don't know where the water's coming from," Solo is saying. "But it's clean."

"I thought you lived in the mines."

"The mines are below us. They're damp. Jazzie, we'd be foolish to live there."

"How do you get the mafinite?"

"We're connected to the mines. I'll show you later."

Jasmin looks around, there's not much comfort here. Clothes are hanging off hooks on wooden beams. Logs from the ground hold the roof. Solo, attentive to Jasmin's observation, explains: 'Moisture in the air swells the timber to make a solid lock.'

Jasmin tries to sit up, but there's a gong in her head. She collapses with a groan.

"Please rest," says Solo. "You've been out all this time."

"How long."

"Two days and a bit." Solo touches her forehead. "The fever has loosened."

"Two days?" croaks Jasmin.

The children, she thinks. Godi.

* * *

She's still weak on her feet. She uses a bucket full of warm water someone has prepared to wash herself in an open-doored enclosure outside the cave, watched under the moonlit night by a cow, a bull, a calf, three cockerels—two russet and one murky—and eight black and white flecked hens.

She wanders with a slight limp to the creek. There's acid in her legs from all that running, that climbing. Speckled fish roll and leap in the clean water's pulse, a luminous trail in their tail fins.

Solo introduces the cows. "Moosa, Dusk and Buttercup."

Moosa is golden brown with a wet black nose and big black eyes. Dusk is the velvet black of a moonless night, her yellow eyes warm as sunshine. Buttercup is white and gray with a gentle black face, capped with a silvery patch that reminds one of a fascinator.

"Where did you get them?"

"Rescues, before Mafinga made corpses of the rest. The mothers died, but their calves made it. Now they're full grown. Moosa gives us milk. And the hens lay eggs daily."

Solo pulls a pair of clean overalls and a flannel shirt off a hook on the wooden beam just inside the cave. Hands them to Jasmin. "You'll need these."

"What happened to . . ."

"That shit you were wearing is foul. Someone's cleaning it for you."

They find her thick socks and fuck-off boots, thick as an insult.

"What are you up to with all this?" Jasmin gestures with her hands, indicates the camp.

"We're rebuilding Mafinga. This is the future."

"And who does the mines?"

"We take turns. If the mafinite keeps showing at the castle, the king and Atari have no clue or don't care about what else is going on." She points at a stack of wooden crates. "We're also making weapons."

Jasmin opens a crate. "Knives, drills, spades and catapults? How will these fare against the guards and their tasers, their lasers?"

"We have the numbers. There are fifteen of us. The guards— maybe four?"

"I took out Maridadi. That leaves the guard in the castle, perhaps two more in the shuttle."

"And the factory supervisors?"

"Hotel is on our side. Thrifty not so much. There are also traitors, counting Ten and Abebe. But Atari is the real threat."

They join the circle around a modest fire at the cave's entrance. It's semiarid outside, but Jasmin can see sprouts of new grass growing, ripe green-yellow blades shooting from the reddish-brown soil.

"We move the animals to let the grass grow," says Solo. "But we never take them too far to graze. Out here is a whole new world to explore. And it's all part of Mafinga."

Jasmin looks around the gathered community. They are all dressed in mine gear. Pale khaki overalls, flannel shirts with red and white squares. Thick boots. All but Solo are hesitant around her, a newcomer, even though they once worked together at Ujamaa Factory.

"We take shifts," says Solo. "Some work in the mines, as the rest tend to the future of Mafinga. Come," she grabs Jasmin's hand, "let's introduce you."

"That's Barricade," Solo points.

Jasmin remembers the woman—she was a floor supervisor at the factory. Now she's sprawled by the fire, wearing about her more sense of entitlement than an infant. But she's no infant. She's a big girl, bush-browed, square-jawed. She's sitting with earmuffs on, the kind you get in the mines, cracking the fingers of her big-knuckled hands. Jasmin nods at her.

"Fuck off, yeah," says Barricade. She lifts the earmuffs. "You know what's in a shift."

"What?"

"A big fat *F*."

The rest of them laugh.

Barricade blocks off her hearing again, removes herself from camaraderie.

Petal has a small face, tiny stature. She's wearing a silver ring on her nose. "Going good?" She seems the obliging sort. Smiles at Jasmin to reveal a silver cap on her upper incisor.

"Swell."

"Don't disregard her small size," says Solo. "Small as that one is, wait until you see her shoveling rock."

Zed is harried-looking, pepper and salt on her short crop. She turns her beleaguered face away from Jasmin's nod.

"Strong as a bull, that one too," says Solo. "Drills like a demon."

Bo has big ears and a brood mouth. She's a "never there," you hardly notice her. Her feet are tiny in the fuck-off boots.

"Bo's the important person," says Solo. "She's the winder driver—manages the cage."

"I didn't see a cage," says Jasmin.

"You will if you go to the mines. It takes four people at a time, an intimate squeeze. You need tolerance of people around here."

"Tell that to Barricade."

Petal is stoking the fire, setting it up with a mesh on stands for a barbecue.

"Where do you get the meat?" asks Jasmine.

"Ground hogs wander around. But just look at what's on the spit."

It's skewers of crucified lizards on a sizzle. A waft of burnt sugar and smoke, a crackle of fat, in the air. Petal adds pieces of tubular meat that's all sinewy, full of bones, when Jasmin bites into it.

"Your first rattlesnake," says Solo midchew.

Jasmin makes a face. "The lizards carry more taste."

"Now you just hold on," says Solo. She goes into the cave, comes out with a dry reed. She crushes it with a stone, sprinkles it on the roasted snake. It adds a seaweed taste to the meat. "Don't get used to it—this is our guest special."

Jasmin smiles.

"It's not always meat," says Solo, "although every now and then there's a roast of cave beetles. They crunch like nuts. There's milk and eggs, but we go sparing on those. The food cache is mostly dried, we're saving it for Mafinga. Right here is everything we need for a new beginning."

Jasmin looks at the miners, no ounce of fat on them.

"We eat fern, moss, spleenwort, nettle, liverworts," says Solo. "It's a food chain. Bat poop is good."

"To eat?"

"For the plants," says Solo.

"And the fish?"

"We've never eaten the fish."

Petal seats herself between Jasmin and Solo. "We hear you're from the castle."

"That's no badge of honor."

"Be nice, Jasmin," chides Solo. "Petal and Zed are the ones who saved you, rang the bell to get the crew. We communicate by bell when we leave the camp, go to Ujamaa Village or the mines."

"It's a code of signals," says Petal. "The first thing a trainee learns when the system assigns them to the mines."

"In answer to your question, my stay at the castle was as the queen's prisoner," says Jasmin. "Technically, I still am captive."

"Why is that?" asks Petal.

"My children are there."

"Did the sorcerer Atari treat you right?" jokes Petal.

"He's no sorcerer," says Jasmin. "He's empty as a fart, and just as foul."

"And the bitch of a queen is right there to do his bidding."

"She's not a bitch!"

The camp falls into silence. All eyes are on Jasmin who's astonished by her defense of the woman who's taken her husband, the very woman holding Mia and Omar hostage. But even that's an unfair depiction. No one can cleanly portray the conditions of Mia and Omar's keep at the castle as anything near hostage. Enamored as they are with Queen Sheeba, climbing her at whim, the true hostage is most likely the queen.

4

"It's cooler out here compared to the rest of Mafinga." Jasmin diffuses the tension.

"Mafinga was always hot," says Solo. "It became unbearable without trees or shelter."

"Once we have it, our new beginning," says Jasmin, "Godi will do his magic on the land."

Solo laughs. "Our *insider*—he's a good find. We must go in soon, bring the animals before the sun comes out."

"There's nothing wrong with the sun." Gasps of astonishment, then indignation. "It's all a mind game. Atari's behind it."

"Explains the fish, we always wondered why they weren't dying under the sun when everything else did. It's why we never ate them."

"Really?"

"Before each dawn we brought in the cows and the chicken, but the fish kept swimming."

"What about all those men who died?" asks Petal.

"The supplements, toxic." Jasmin looks at them. "Something else you must know. The king is dying."

What she was expecting is not this—a burst of ululation that overwhelms all sound.

* * *

Jasmin works out a plan. "I'll return to the castle," she says. "Buy time as your people gather the rest of the miners and group their weapons."

"My people? I know you love me, Jazzie, but you should know me better. You think I'll stand by as others fight?"

"Of course, I know you! You won't be doing nothing, Solo. You'll go to Ujamaa Village, band the people. Join me at the castle and we'll deal with Atari."

"And the guards?"

"I thought you wanted to fight. How many guards against what— fifteen of you?"

"Counting the ones in the mines."

"Where are the mines?" asks Jasmin.

"Hundreds of meters below. The mafinite is embedded in volcanic rock that sometimes climbs to the surface. We extract it and wash it. Take it up the cage in a mine truck. Come with me, I'd like to show you something."

Jasmin follows her into the lit cave entrance and into its throat. Light fades inward as they go into the cavern until they arrive at a pit. Solo opens a gate marked "No Entry Zone."

"There are eight people in the mines right now."

"How do you know?"

"The dog tags," she points. "You have to leave each one, lettered with your initials, when you go into the mines. You collect it on exit. This way we know where people are."

Jasmin looks at the solid structure facing her. "The mine cage."

"It takes four miners at a time. Works on an alternating pulley. Two minutes, and you're in the mines. We put broken rock in the mine trucks, bring them up the cage too. The winding engine is inside the cavern. It uses compressed air. Bo, our winder, moves the levers to rotate the wheels that move the cage. A dial shows her what level in the mines the cage is located. She sends and releases it at a bell code. Each mining level has a code. A single bell means stop. Two bells, a pause and then three means it's a request to bring the cage to level five."

"You don't want to piss off the winder driver," says Jasmin.

"No, you don't."

Solo shows Jasmin a compartment. "Here is the change room. Mostly for the miners to fetch a hard hat, waist battery for the head lamp and the harness. You wear the strapping at all times, even in the cage, lest there's malfunction and you must take the escape route through the ladder."

"How is the quality of air in the mines?"

"Natural ventilation. It's simple: hot air rises. Sometimes the mines get very hot and full of dust, especially after drilling. Miners take a break as the mine self-cleanses." Solo fondles Jasmin's cheek. "You want to take the cage, see what I do for a living?"

"Are you suggesting a quick romp in the mines?"

"You know me too well. You'll have to wear the harness."

"That sounds quite kinky," husk in Jasmin's voice, "especially when you also wear gloves. But skip the mines, I'll take you right here."

She snaps the press buttons on Solo's overalls. Unbuttons the front of the shirt under which Solo is without a bra. Jasmin fondles the firm swell of milk chocolate breasts tipped with nipples dark as mousse. She runs her tongue over each, bites gently.

"Someone will find us," pleads Solo, but her hands are pressing Jasmin's head to stay. She moans as Jasmin's lips find hers.

* * *

They return to the cave's entrance splashed with moonlight. Jasmin averts her gaze from the women's curiosity. She wonders if her buttons are askew, her overalls all tousled. Somehow, she feels ashamed. She looks at Solo who's wearing a silly grin. Barricade makes a donkey sound—an obscene bray. Petal picks up the bray, then shifts it to grunting. Wolf whistles all round, then a burst of ribald laughter.

"Stop it already now," says Solo. "Back to work, right."

Jasmin smiles. She understands the women's acceptance of her. She senses some sort of deference. They appear to treat Solo as their leader.

"Let's get you back into that Heidi number," says Solo. "You'd create commotion rocking up to the castle in those overalls."

There's nothing fresh smelling about the dress, just the crispness of a wash and the kind of press you get from putting a cloth between two stones. It's fully creased along the folds, but it's better than the puke-splattered garb of before.

They trudge inwards, carefully through uneven surface with broken rock, toward darkness, away from the cave's entrance. The walk is tricky.

"Maybe you could get the crew to find Maridadi?" suggests Jasmin. "Her carcass will stink the place down."

"The vultures will do a number on her. Cave critters will finish the rest."

They arrive at a wall.

"It's a dead end," says Jasmin.

"No." Solo finds a lever tucked beneath a rock. She pulls it and the wall grinds to an angle.

Jasmin remembers this place—it's the fork of dread where she kept getting lost. She shudders at the thought of passing the maw that took Maridadi. But they never reach it. They keep walking until they get to another wall, another lever. It opens to a way that leads to familiar stalactites: multicoloreds, whites and yellow-browns.

"We part here," says Solo. "Go east until you reach the castle's cellar door. I take the west leg. Unless—?"

"I'll be fine, Solo. I don't need you to come with me."

"If they ask at the castle, where will you say you've been?"

"I got lost?"

"That usually works. You might need to say a bit more to account for being lost three days."

"I'll be fine, Solo. How do you get into Ujamaa Village?"

"Mama Gambo's unit. Right inside."

"But there are eyes everywhere."

"We tinkered with the cameras."

"How many insiders do you have?"

"You'd be astonished to know."

Which of the Tech teenagers is it? wonders Jasmin. Junkie, the one with spiked hair, was quietest.

"You hesitate, my love. Are you sure you'll be fine on your own?"

"You know the adage: Alone, you go fast."

"But what about the proverb: Together, you go far?"

"Yours is an important task, Solo. Group our friends at Ujamaa Village. It's time we claimed our country. Put a stop to the nonsense."

They cling to each other one last time.

5

Jasmin approaches the wooden door of the cellar with a rise of panic. Before she left the castle, neither she nor Godi thought or had time to work out a code of signals like the one of the mines. They could have come up with two knocks to say *hello*. Three knocks to say *it's Jasmin*. Two knocks, pause, three. If Godi misunderstood, he'd knock back once. And she'd repeat the signal. Then he'd answer back with his own code. Two knocks to say *hello*. Five knocks to say *it's Godi*. Two knocks, pause, five. And she'd be back inside, safe in Godi's arms.

Without a signal, she doesn't know what's behind the door. She doesn't know if Godi is waiting, and that blasted fever got in the way. Jasmin has been away from the castle for days. Her absence is surely noticed. She remembers the folktale of Ali Baba whose unthinking brother got stuck inside the den because he forgot the words to release the door. All he had to do was say, *"Open Sesame!"*

Instead, he uselessly chanted:

"Open Samosa!"

"Open Simbisi!"

"Open Satshuma!"

Nothing happened. The den stayed shut with him locked inside. When the forty thieves returned, they killed him with sabers, quartered him and nailed him up to the cave wall.

Jasmin arrives at the wooden door. She raises a shaky hand, raps twice. Three raps come back, loud and clear. The sound of a bolt slithering back. The groan of a hinge, as the door swings inward.

"Oh, Godi. I thought—"

She falls straight into Atari. The sight of him drowns her with dread. His monstrous head on a child's body, big bones pushing against his skin like a malignant cancer. Up close, she is repulsed by his luminescent skin. His cold grip on her arms before she can think to run is as solid as steel. She fights to get away, pushing and dragging, kicking and twisting.

"We have been waiting," he says calmly. "You can nout get away."

As Jasmin wonders at the plurality of his words—who's "we"?—something cracks at her head.

* * *

She comes to, slowly, gets her bearing. She's on a floor, trussed like a pig. There's a smell of burning, an acridity that stings her eyes, her nose. She recognizes the vat in the middle, its height of a person, its width that takes half the room. She's in Atari's lab.

It must have been in the mind—the headiness she'd previously felt in the lab when she was in fright of a golem. It's nonexistent now. Her head is clear. She's filled with survival instinct. She looks around. She sees a guard by the door. Atari by the vat.

"Jas." She sees Godi on the floor, bound up like a goat with ropes. "I'm sorry," he says. "I've failed you, the children."

"Don't talk that way, Godi. Help is coming. The queen?"

"I don't know. I waited for you, my Jas, two nights. I was planning to come out to the mines on the third, but Atari was onto me."

Her heart swells with something bigger than herself at the sight of him so helpless on the floor, his hood gone. She looks at his white hair, the disfigurement on his face, and she knows that she loves him. He is her Betelgeuse, the brightest in her sky. But something tells her she must make him the second brightest in her constellation. Uncertainty is their new mantra; he can no more be her sanctuary. His ribs rise and fall. Every element in her core chants to the rhythm of his breathing. He moves his body, so they are facing each other. His gaze is directly upon her, dawn-gray eyes that shift to a blue-green gray the more he looks at her.

She opens her lips to say words full of meaning, closes them in silence. To speak of her feelings will break the spell. It doesn't seem long how much she has with him, how much longer he can be hers in this moment. There's a clear distinction between her longing and their need, her thirst for his kiss full of wilderness and the certainty of what should matter now. Theirs will remain a spiritual connection, perhaps enriching other lives.

Mafinga must find rescue. Perhaps Jasmine's death, Godi's too, is the sacrifice Mafinga needs to liberate herself. Jasmine craves giant shoulders to contain the beat of her racing heart. She's on the clock. Godi's on the clock. The intensity of her feelings, of her desire for a future, nearly overwhelms. Any minute now and, surely, she'll explode, leaving a celestial splatter as she turns into a black hole.

"Bring the scar face," says Atari, his voice octaves high.

The guard hauls Godi to his feet.

"Jas," he says. "You're my one-way street, there's no wrong turn."

"Godi!" Jasmin is struggling to free herself. Now she is begging, "Please, Atari. There's no need for harm. I'll do anything, just let him go!" She tries to rise but it's useless, and then it's impossible as strong hands push her to the floor.

"I warned you to stay away from Atari's plans. Now you're more than a threat." It's Abebe.

Jasmin spits at the woman's face. "You can't condemn us without a hearing."

"It looks as if you're offering yourself up for a new trial," says Abebe. "We're going to accept it. Only this time it won't be the queen as your judge. And your judgment is already spoken."

"Not if I can help it," says the queen's faraway voice.

She smashes the back of Abebe's skull with the branch of a tree. Abebe crumbles to the floor. Queen Sheeba's eyes are wild, her breathing rapid. "Locking me in my room was very stupid. I always keep spares."

It all happens so quickly. One second the queen is untying Jasmin's knots, but the guard is rushing at them, only she doesn't know what to do when she reaches the queen who's still a monarch. The guard grabs Jasmin, her ropes falling.

"Let her go at once," commands the queen in her distant voice. The guard looks uncertain.

"I am your queen and I'm commanding you to stand down."

"You're nout to do anything of the kind," says Atari in his squeak. The guard is still hesitant.

"I am the king's right hand. Your job is to obey me," says Atari.

"The king is dying," says Queen Sheeba. "I'm your queen and the people of the resistance are coming. It's all over now. Let her go. I said at once!"

In that moment of hesitation, Jasmin elbows the guard in the ribs, lands a headbutt. The guard lets go. Jasmin swirls, rams the guard's socket with her right elbow. The guard staggers backward, reaching for the taser strapped on her belt. They wrestle. The guard is taller, stronger. Jasmin is in a chokehold. She trips the guard, throws a punch that connects with the head and the guard drops.

Jasmin falls on the guard with her full weight, striking repeatedly on the head with her fists, her elbows, anything that can hit, that can hurt. She was never a fighter—it's all instinct and survival, her children and Godi behind her rage. She hits until it feels her own bones are breaking. The guard is immobile. Jasmin grabs the taser.

Atari is shoving Godi toward the mad boil of the vat.

Jasmin wields the taser with both hands, points it at the horror head. "I warn you, let him go."

Atari pushes Godi closer to the raging vat. Passion, dread and adrenaline rush Jasmin forward. She lowers the device toward Atari's chest, presses the activation button. She sees and hears sparks as twin wires shoot out in an arc at speed. Atari releases Godi, leaps to the side from the tethered electrodes. Godi falls away from the vat. Jasmin pounces on Atari, presses the end of the taser to his neck, pushes the button. She holds, unsure if the device will work twice so close. It does, and it's a direct hit like an electric prod. She holds for seconds on the translucent skin with a pale green hue as Atari flops and shakes, then she pulls away.

She rolls back, overcome with emotions that are too many to isolate.

To her left, Queen Sheeba is unroping Godi.

His first instinct surprises them—he reaches for Jasmin. Eases the gun from her hands, puts it to safety and sweeps her into his arms. He rocks her, saying the same words over and over. "Two ants will pull a grasshopper."

She's wrapped in their chemistry, her body soft in his arms. She speaks against him. 'Solo and the others are on the way.'

"Watch out," says the queen. "The alien is coming to."

And so he is.

Atari is laughing, rising to height. He's fully recovered but for the bruise on his neck.

* * *

He laughs at the scene that opens before him—the ending that's nearly a beginning. Doors that won't open, won't stay closed. How will this threesome work out if they live to what's next, manage not to die? He's never seen this kind of affection, never saw it in his parents. His father was cold as frost—his lips mostly straight as the stars of Orion. His mother wore the scent of a salty oasis—as a child he only smelled it from a distance. She kept him locked up in a nursery. His parents were never made of kindness. Their love was a selfish one of two.

But this new scene before his eyes shows him the perfection of a trinity: three people who will die for each other. The scar face with his mind of Einstein—his brain ticking, even as the odds pile against him. The queen and her quiet strength, beauty of a planet that eats up light. The persistent girl who defies the laws of physics or science of the mind—she keeps coming back despite her fear. The impossibility of this trinity confounds him.

It's a completeness in three he'd never thought possible. Not after his parents—they were incapable of it. Why else could they never accept him? He was not ever enough as an only child. Why was he never complete for them? But he looks at three people before him and laughs with satisfaction at the realization of his ideology.

Three is enough. Each third is integral to the equation.

Atari hears the girl say: "How much voltage does it take to knock this one?"

* * *

Atari's laughter startles Jasmin. It's the cough of a polecat, or something dying.

"How much voltage does it take to knock this one—" she begins. She is reaching for the taser, but Godi beats her to it.

And then it's mayhem. An angry throng bursts into the lab.

As the crowd flows, Atari, giggling madly, leaps to his feet. He escapes toward the far end of the lab's circular dome.

But a murder of women—Solo, Barricade, Petal, Bo, Mama Gambo, Hotel, Apiyo and the rest—pounces on him.

DENOUEMENT

1

Queen Sheeba is wearing a flowing maxi tunic of pure silk and charmeuse. It drapes sensually over her full hips. Each time she waves a hand in gesture, her wrist flashes with the multipearl bracelet, ornamented with white gold and diamonds. Now she's seated on her throne inside the courthouse. To each side of her on the dais are Jasmin, Solo, Godi, Mama Gambo and Apiyo, her assigned advisers for the grave matter at hand.

The audience is from the mines and Ujamaa Village—these ones mostly looking about and gaping, dazzled by magnificence.

Today the queen takes the cascading-heart tiara off herself, no guard or servant to do it. She seems uncertain what to do with the crown now it's off her head. Jasmin relieves her of it, places it under her seat.

The queen dons a black cloth on her head to conduct the solemn hearing. She speaks quietly. "This is a trial by the people," she says to the gathering. "I pass on the wand of the courthouse to the advisers seated here before you by my side."

Jasmin rises and speaks to the people. "Atari is a murderer. He has killed your husbands. Your sons. He has achieved much evil, thanks to the company of these lapwings." She beckons toward Abebe and the three captured guards, each one well roughed up.

"Baboons don't go far from their tree," says Mama Apiyo.

"Atari, I speak to you," says Jasmin. "Have you anything to say

192 · EUGEN BACON

before we pronounce judgment? Perhaps you might explain to us your vision, the ideology in interpretation and that which you implemented in Mafinga. In your mind, has villagization and a servitude attitude pushed us toward an ideal society of national unity?"

Solemn as a golem, he looks straight ahead.

"And the rest of you—you were channels of the people's emotional and physical destruction. How do you plead?"

"Not guilty. I insist you let me go," says Abebe in her funereal dress. "If you're removing hyenas from a pit, I'm not one of them. I have served the queen faithfully."

"As you have served Atari," says Jasmin.

"Let me attest to that," says the queen.

"You do not judge a person for their misfortune," says Abebe. "I did not choose to be a servant. You will understand that I had no choice than to obey the king's right hand."

Jasmin looks at the guards. "And you—do you have anything to say?"

"We were just following orders."

"The way Maridadi followed hers to massacre Violet?" asks Mama Apiyo gently. "I rest my case."

"It's simple," says Mama Gambo. "When poisoned arrows have not entered too deeply, removing them is not too hard."

"And how do you propose we remove the arrows?" asks the queen.

"A simple hanging for these four," says Mama Gambo. "One was a servant, three were obeying orders. As for that one, leave it to me to deliberate and decide on his judgment. You will accept it?"

"If anyone is to claim justice, it's Mama Gambo," says Jasmin.

"I agree," says Godi.

"I agree," says Solo.

"I agree," says Mama Apiyo.

"Hear, hear," chants the crowd.

"It is decided," says the queen.

Abebe—starved to hear pardon, now denied—gasps at this, then groans. She throws herself to the ground, tears her hair and begins to wail. Her cry is at intervals, the screech of a barred owl. The weeping transforms to sorrowful lyrics about innocuous observers forced into unpaid duty, now no one is there to defend their case. But she composes herself on time to ask if there might be a last supper.

Jasmin sends Petal who goes running to the camp to fetch milk and eggs, even a fistful of cave beetles for roasting.

As the court session ends, a ripple in the audience beginning to move, Solo puts an arm around Jasmin's shoulder. "You're taking over my people."

"You mean Petal? That was just a chore."

"How quickly she obeyed—it was more than a chore. We have a new leader."

Jasmin shakes her head. "The queen—she's the ruler."

"Is she really?"

They look at each other.

Just then a villager poses a question to the queen and her scatter of advisers on the dais.

"But what about the children?" asks the villager, at which Jasmin nearly collapses. "The ones in Tech," elaborates the questioner, and Jasmin finds some composure. For a moment she imagined in her dread that her children were in peril. Shaken, she still can't trust herself to be steady.

The queen looks at Jasmin as if only she knows the answer. Then she looks at the rest.

"You cannot blame the pot when the cassava turns out bland," begins Jasmin slowly. "And I believe there may have been inside help from Tech to disarm some overhead cameras."

"Yes," agrees Godi. "The teenagers can be rehabilitated. We'll put their cleverness to the real good of the people this time."

* * *

Nobody in Mafinga is skilled to do a hanging. There's rope in Ujamaa Canteen, but what kind is right? How does one tell if it's too thin, too fat, too long, too short? And one rope doesn't fit all. Then, once you get the right rope, who knows to do the noose, and do it right?

Two tries for the first guard, she doesn't fall unconscious. She makes noises for fifteen minutes and it is Barricade with her earmuffs who cuts her down.

"This is a big fat *F*," she says.

Bo helps her redo the rope. This time the guard takes ten minutes, and a Samaritan strikes her on the head with a rock to knock her out before they hang her a fourth successful time.

The rope is too long for the second guard's weight, and her head snaps and lolls, squirting blood from the torn neck to the feet of the observers. Its eyes are rolled into pupils open wide with terror, mouth gaping in a silent scream, causing a stampede.

The branch breaks on the third guard, and they must hook her back on another branch of the star tree with olive leaves. She jerks on the rope for eight minutes and a half before she goes still. They get it right by the time they reach Abebe.

By then they realize too late that they'd forgotten to shield her from the previous hangings, and she'd witnessed them all. People turn away as volunteers steer her out to the hanging tree, because she has long loosened her bowels. She stays numbed with the shock all the way to the tree, even as she drops to a clean hanging. She's dead in four minutes, witnessed by the castle's Ujamaa monuments of togetherness, sculpted hands of a village holding aloft a toddler.

2

A crowd is more than the sum of its parts and when it is an execution, it's more than the syncopation of embodied justice. Does a killing scrape the harm of more names carved in gravestones, nothing about blood or memory, just surface words that are dissonance between what is real and the ideal? Does anyone ever write: *He was a real jerk, untidy to the core. Fucked like a dog. Smelled like a rat, thank gods he's dead?* A crowd is a finger in the eye of your shame, up yours. You die before you get there, wherever you're destined to be. The tears on your face as you swing on the rope.

A crowd is watching. Atari hates crowds. He hated when it rushed at him, when hands touched him, and confirmed to him everything he hates about crowds. They snarl, they grunt, the floor shakes with their tremors like an aftershock. There's no dignity in a crowd.

Their fake hearing—a trial by the people? It's a little ironic that they have fully embraced the Ujamaa concept. Together, they are, good for each other and working in a unit. Together, they are, rejecting him. He's amused that they will not hang him like the others. Their legs trembled as Hyphen's did when he croaked.

They should have hanged him, he would have died—choking will do it. Now he imagines it will be death by a thousand cuts. Cut out his head, put it between his knees as they did to that one who ran the canteen.

He flinches as many hands seize him. He tries to warn them what will happen if they tear him in their rage. He regenerates. There'd be a minion of Atari siblings kicking about, and Mafinga doesn't want that to happen—those creatures are all flawed. Atari is the only perfect version of himself.

Nobody is listening. Nobody cares. He is airborne.

He realizes too late the crowd is shuffling for the vat that's madly boiling. "Nout! Nout!" He squeals at a lick of molten bubble on his skin from the vat's fury. "Nout!"

The lava is a parasite. An autosite that will harvest him, steal his heart, his brain. It will absorb him in the cavern like a vanishing twin. "Nout!"

The lava is very hungry. It gurgles and swallows his scream.

3

Queen Sheeba looks at Jasmin. "What will you do now?"

"Such calamity it would have been had Sylvia Pathos listened to old brays of the heart but never written a single let alone final word," says Jasmin.

"The author Maddison," says the queen.

"Godi has introduced you to our storytellers."

"Yes. That's right—*your* storytellers," says the queen. "I've never been able to claim him, you see. Godi."

He turns at his name. "What's that?"

"Nothing," says the queen. "Woman talk." She directs her question to Jasmin. "So, will you write the rest of the narrative?"

"With the people, yes. We must take agency for our story. Rebuild Mafinga. The husk of it." Jasmin looks at Godi, "As you did with the gardens—can you fix it?"

"I'll do my best," he says. "Restring, retune the story. Be an apt listener for a . . . what's the word? Muse."

"Our thinking shapes who we become. You have all the muse you need—after all, you're . . . Tolkien?"

"And I should write for the world?"

"Just for Mafinga." Jasmin turns to the queen. "And you? What will you do?"

"The king is still dying." She smiles sadly. "I'll see him to his end. I loved his father dearly, and I owe him that. But there's much reparation to fix the damage Atari has done. The castle, the mines—there's enough wealth to reconstruct our country. We might get more mafinite when we drain the vat. Heaven knows why Atari chose to make a liquid of the gemstone. It's clear that he drank it, but why?"

"What if it was a drug, some sort of addiction?" jokes Jasmin. The three of them laugh at the impossibility of the idea. Jasmin goes serious. "You would give up the castle?"

"I don't need to live in luxury at the expense of the people. Happiness comes simple." She looks at Godi.

For Jasmin, it's bittersweet. There's never a happy ending. She deserves a good ending. "And what happens to the uranium?"

"I'm not sure it's a blessing or a growing problem. There must be safe ways to mine it."

"What if I say we leave it alone," says Jasmin. "That we don't touch the uranium."

"I will listen," says the queen. "But I'm sure you'll tell me the thinking behind your reasoning."

"Why cost ourselves more? Let's not be the vultures that land on our village. There's been enough destruction to Mafinga. It makes no sense to further damage the earth, our land."

"I agree. We'll use the remaining mafinite to recompense the people. We can only hope the miners will stay on task—better remuneration, of course." She looks at Jasmin. "But something tells me Solo may not be one of those to remain in the mines?"

"Maybe, maybe not. We'll have to rebuild Ujamaa Village. The units are as good as prison cells."

"Of course. Anything you need."

Godi intercepts their conversation. "I hope you don't mind if I take Jasmin away from you."

"By all means," says the queen.

He takes Jasmin's hand. His touch is full of stars.

"Let me walk with you. The children are eagerly waiting to see you."

"As am I."

Outside, the sky is quickly changing. It sheds its black cloak as a bright orange-red sun begins to rise. Jasmin raises her face to the horizon in awe. She had forgotten how perfect the sun makes her feel. She's calm and focused, a warm blush on her cheeks.

She walks with Godi in silence until they enter the main castle. He faces her squarely, clasps her hands in his. "I don't like it about Solo any more than you do about Sheeba."

Jasmin doesn't know what to say. That Solo is the solvent in Jasmin's language of water?

Godi's grip tightens, his eyes full of worry. "There's something you should know." He avoids her gaze.

"Don't tell me Sheeba is pregnant."

"Jas . . ."

"You're not joking." She looks at him in shock.

"That tells me how you feel about the matter."

"It might be a constant battle. But I can live with it."

"Are you sure?"

"No."

Now the queen's earlier words make more sense. *The terror each time you fall pregnant.* How she clutched her stomach, looked about to throw up. *Thinking that this child will also die.* How much does Godi know?

"Godi." She touches his arm. "Sheeba has lost babies. It's not an easy thing. A pregnancy is not—"

"A guarantee? I know."

He draws her to an embrace. She presses against him, his sweet smell of books.

"Can I kiss you?" he whispers into her hair. "One last time?"

"No, my tall plushie. First, one never asks to kiss a woman."

Every inch of her yearns for his wilderness taste one more time. The tenderness and urgency of his lips. "Second, I'll not give you a new memory. You have enough old ones to last a lifetime. And we'll always be family. Always."

They hold on to each other a moment longer. Reluctantly, she pulls away.

"Is this the end, my Jas?"

She laughs, but there's a deep sense of loss. "It's only a beginning."

She feels his eyes as she walks away, now she's running. She races up the winding staircase, hands moving along its mahogany rail shimmering with sheen. She rushes up a flight, up another, up, up. She climbs with such thrill, such rush, all the way to the nursery. She flings herself into the rotary room. There's Mia in her unicorn pajama set, tiny shorts and a T-shirt. There's Omar in his all-over flying dragons. They are lying on the floor, head-to-head, as the nursery spins.

"My goatlings."

Mia puckers up at the sight of her. Omar's eyes are full of reproach.

"You've missed three story times, Mama."

She drops to her knees, throws her arms wide open and the children fall into them.

"Mama."

"Mamm. I good, Mamm, aight?"

Jasmin chokes that Mia might have thought her absence was a reprimand. "You're always, always good, my love." These two are her reason to love, her heartbeat to live.

"Roar," says Omar against her chest. "I'm a dragon. Let me breathe you some fire."

Jasmin wrestles him to the ground, and he squeals. Mia throws herself upon them, she too squealing.

Morning is here. Jasmin takes her children by the hands. They skip together down the stairs, leaping onto each landing.

"Wheee!"

"Wheee!"

"Wheee!"

They rush to the doorway of the castle. Mia and Omar pause, uncertain at the threshold.

"Go on, my goatlings."

Jasmin takes their hands. Together, they step out into the wonderment of the sun.

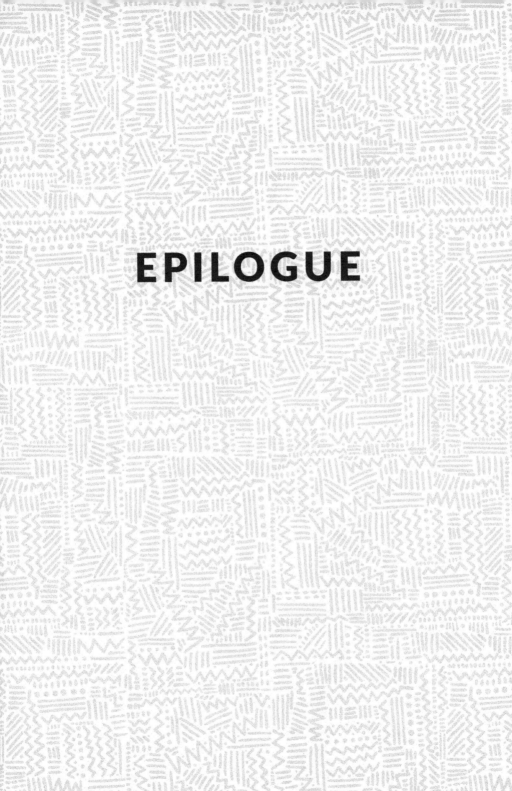

EPILOGUE

Praxis or regimen is especially hard to give up.

The people of Mafinga are ensconced in the courthouse with its floor to ceiling windows. Someone has untangled the melancholy ribbons that bound the golden drapes, so they now fall from their hourglass shapes to straight curtains that cloak the crowd from dawn.

But there's something called curiosity.

People spill one by one and pour out onto the castle's bloodred flowers and a new break of day, arms out, eyes squinting at the sun.

The end. But, no—is a story truly finished?

Soon it will be night and we'll be shadows embossed against the tall, black rectangle of a doorway. Right there at the threshold of an in or out, in the heartbeat of a northeast soaker that washes in reason, we will stare at fate and wonder what happens to the people of Mafinga now. To Jasmin, Solo, Godi and Sheeba. To Mia, Omar, Mama Gambo and the rest.

And what happened to Gretel after her role in killing the witch, to the pied piper after she took the children of Hamelin, to Briar Rose on the morning after, month after, year after . . . her marriage to the prince?

But there are also ardent questions about the nature of story— what it does to an individual.

The non-end.

ACKNOWLEDGMENTS

To the publisher Tricia Reeks of Meerkat Press.
   For your passion and belief.

To Bieke van Aggelen of the African Literary Agency.
   For walking this book's journey.

ABOUT THE AUTHOR

Eugen M. Bacon is African Australian, a computer scientist mentally re-engineered into creative writing. Her novella *Ivory's Story* was shortlisted in the 2020 British Science Fiction Association Awards. Her work has won, been shortlisted, longlisted or commended in national and international awards, including the Foreword Book of the Year Awards, Bridport Prize, Copyright Agency Prize, Australian Shadows Awards, Ditmar Awards and Nommo Awards for Speculative Fiction by Africans.

Bacon's creative work has appeared in literary and speculative fiction publications worldwide, including *Aurealis*, *Australian Anthology of Prose Poetry*, *Award Winning Australian Writing*, *Fantasy Magazine*, *Fantasy & Science Fiction*, Dark Moon Books, British Science Fiction Association, *LitHub*, *Unsung Stories*, Bloomsbury Publishing, through Routledge in *New Writing* and *The Year's Best African Speculative Fiction*. Recent books: *Danged Black Thing*, Transit Lounge Publishing (2021), *Mage of Fools*, Meerkat Press (2022) and *Chasing Whispers*, Raw Dog Screaming Press (2022).

Website: eugenbacon.com / **Twitter:** @EugenBacon

DID YOU ENJOY THIS BOOK?

If so, word-of-mouth recommendations and online reviews are critical to the success of any book, so we hope you'll tell your friends about it and consider leaving a review at your favorite bookseller's or library's website.

Visit us at www.meerkatpress.com for our full catalog.

Meerkat Press
Asheville